HERMANN ABERT

MOZART'S DON GIOVANNI

HERMANN ABERT

MOZART'S

Don Giovanni

TRANSLATED BY
PETER GELLHORN

EULENBURG BOOKS
LONDON

Originally published in German by Breitkopf & Härtel, Wiesbaden.

This edition first published in 1976 by
Ernst Eulenburg Ltd., 48 Great Marlborough Street, London W1V 2BN.

Reprinted 1981

ISBN 0 903873 19 2 (hardback)
     0 903873 11 7 (paperback)

Printed in Great Britain by Page Bros (Norwich) Ltd.

CONTENTS

Translator's Preface   7

Mozart in Prague   9

Don Giovanni   26

TRANSLATOR'S PREFACE

Hermann Abert entirely rewrote the passages dealing with *Don Giovanni* in Otto Jahn's *Mozart*, when he took charge of the sixth edition of this famous book, published by Breitkopf & Härtel in 1924. The great merit of Abert's essay on *Don Giovanni* lies in the way he presents Mozart as a dramatist of incomparable psychological insight. We are not only given an analysis of the general achievement, of the inventive felicities to be found in the score, or of the many instances of brilliant characterization — although in that respect the scrupulous completeness of the essay is impressive and admirable. But Abert also demonstrates that the most exciting aspect of this kind of study is in the attempt to find out how a composer's mind works, to discover the motives that led to the particular way in which he accomplished his task. Here we cannot avoid a certain amount of guesswork; but guesswork, like most other work, can be inspired, and the copious, patient and thorough correlation of evidence, if guided by a sympathetic instinct, can eventually result in live contact with a creative spirit across the centuries. Recent revivals of 17th century music, notably Leppard's adaptations of operas by Monteverdi and Cavalli, have shown how imaginative research and affectionate care can turn an object of musical archaeology into an excellent evening's entertainment, displaying all the wit and psychological appeal of the 'modern' theatre.

By the same token, Abert's illuminations reveal Mozart not only as 'the greatest musician known to me either in person or by name', to quote Haydn's words, but as a powerful creative phenomenon of timeless significance, like Shakespeare or Leonardo, but one whose means of communicating ultimate truths happened to be music.

Not unnaturally, Abert feels obliged to refute some excessively romantic interpretations of the piece, especially as regards certain characters in the story. In this he risks, of course, being taken to task for his own views on the subject. One might argue, for instance, that he sees Leporello too much as a wretched, opportunist little rogue, out for gain and the saving of his own skin, gloating over the discomfiture of his master's victims. The little man could well be seen in a more sympathetic, human light, loyal to Don Giovanni, whom he cannot help admiring, yet disapproving of his conduct which constantly fills him with misgivings, genuinely showing concern for Donna Elvira when he entreats her not to waste her time on such a worthless person, and quite touchingly devoted to his lord at the bitter end, when he tries to avert the oncoming disaster by telling the ghost that Don Giovanni has no time to come to supper, would he please excuse him.

Abert also seems to be a little hard on E.T.A. Hoffmann's contention that Donna Anna is somehow impressed by Don Giovanni, despite her avowed revulsion, and cannot feel at liberty to give her hand to any other man as long as the sinister intruder is alive. Without going to psychological extremes on the subject, the idea seems quite possible and, in the light of Abert's own exposition, certainly within Mozart's scope.

Finally, it would appear that Abert is somewhat unreasonably emphatic in his rejection of Don Ottavio's 'Dalla sua pace' and Donna Elvira's 'Mi tradì', both of which were added later for the first performance in Vienna. Since he agrees that musically they are among Mozart's finest creations, he could hardly deny that they are also eminently suited to the two characters. Ottavio's aria displays the same chivalrous affection that all his other music proclaims, in this case with particular lyric intensity and conviction; Elvira's piece is yet another eloquent testimony to the conflict that divides her against herself: the impassioned determination to be avenged, which in her loving heart turns to pity as soon as the opportunity for revenge arises.

Interesting, and always timely, is Abert's scornful account of the various changes, additions and omissions which producers, conductors, directors and, as Stravinsky would have said, 'other industrialists' have felt impelled to impose on the work to bring it "up to date". It calls to mind Richard Wagner's contention that, far from the opera having to be changed in order to suit the tastes of our time, it is we who are much in need of changing, to be at one with Mozart's creation.

London   Peter Gellhorn
January 1976

MOZART IN PRAGUE

When Mozart returned from his first journey to Prague (1787), he devoted most of his energy to his new opera. After the success of *Figaro* da Ponte appeared to be the obvious librettist. According to his own report he suggested *Don Giovanni* to the composer, who felt extraordinarily attracted to the subject.

Da Ponte tells us in his self-satisfied way how at one and the same time he was arranging Beaumarchais' *Tarare* for Salieri, the *Arbore di Diana* for Martin and *Don Giovanni* for Mozart. In answer to critical remarks from Emperor Joseph II he boldly replied that he would make the attempt: at night he would write for Mozart, which would make him feel as if he were reading Dante's *Inferno*; in the morning for Martin, as if he were studying Petrarch; and in the evening for Salieri, who would be his Tasso. So he set to work, with a bottle of Tokay and a box of Spanish tobacco in front of him, and the pretty daughter of his hostess at his side to inspire him. On the first day, so he says, he wrote the first two scenes of *Don Giovanni*, two scenes of *The Tree of Diana* and more than half the first act of *Tarare*; and after 63 days he had finished the first two operas and written two-thirds of the last.

Unfortunately we learn very little of Mozart's undoubted share in the shaping of the text, or about the progress of the composition in detail. To decide how much of the opera was written while Mozart was still in Vienna and how much in Prague is all the more difficult because we do not know the exact date of his second arrival in Prague. On August 24th, 1787, the day he finished the violin sonata in A major, he was still in Vienna, whereas the contents of his first letter from Prague, dated October 15th, already indicate some prolonged activity in that city. Stiepanek, in the preface to his Czech translation of *Don Giovanni* (1825), puts Mozart's arrival in September; Dlabac, in his Bohemian Dictionary of Artists (1815), asserts that he had spent the whole summer in Prague. Since in Mozart's thematic catalogue no other work follows the A major violin sonata, he probably left Vienna towards the end of August.

If we can rely on da Ponte's account, the libretto must have been completed in June at the latest. Considering Mozart's well-known practice, it is unthinkable that he should not by that time have begun to conceive some of the music. But it is just as true of Mozart as of other composers of that period that the singers engaged in the opera had an important influence on its final shape, particularly in the arias and recitatives; while in ensembles, as we know from *Idomeneo*, Mozart would not allow them to interfere. Therefore he had probably formed a general conception of the music already in Vienna, much of it only in his head, as always; in Prague he would have made alterations and additions to suit the individualities of the singers, and then finally written the score. The precise details will never be known; all one can gather from the letter of October 15th to G. von Jacquin is that the opera was completed earlier than is generally supposed.

Bondini lodged the composer on his arrival at the Three Golden Lions Inn in the Kohlmarkt. His favourite abode, though, was the country house of the Duscheks, the "Bertramka Vineyard", which they had acquired in April, 1784. Long afterwards visitors were shown his room there, as well as the stone table in the garden where he worked at his score while a gay little crowd around him chattered and played billiards.

Naturally a great number of legends surround the origins of *Don Giovanni*. First of all there are the inevitable stories of Mozart's love affairs with his women singers. To what extent they are true we do not know; the manner of their telling smacks of philistine gossip. More important are other reports which show that in the rehearsals Mozart not only supervised the musical side but also directed the stage production. He found that "the company here is not as skilled as the Viennese in studying such an opera in so short a time", but with the mixture of energy, amiability and diplomacy that he showed in such situations he finally achieved his aim. At the beginning of October da Ponte also arrived from Vienna, to be lodged at the back of the Platteis inn, so that poet and composer could comfortably talk to each other through their windows.

The accounts of these rehearsals throw some light not only on Mozart's method, but also on the manner in which an opera was produced in those days. To start with, Luigi Basso had to be calmed down, as he complained that Don Giovanni had no big aria to sing; it is said that Mozart produced five versions of the duet "Là ci darem la mano" before he was finally satisfied. Then Caterina Bondini, the Zerlina, was unwilling to utter the well-known scream in the first Finale. After several vain attempts Mozart himself went on the stage, had the whole passage repeated and at the given moment unexpectedly seized the singer so violently that she screamed in terror. "That is the way!" he said, laughing. We are also told that the words of the Commendatore in the Cemetery scene were originally accompanied only by trombones: but since the players could not bring off the passage to Mozart's satisfaction he asked for the parts and added woodwind instruments.[1] Most important, though, is the fact that according to a trustworthy source, the dinner music in the second Finale was improvised during rehearsals, which would suggest the old opera buffa method.[2]

The first performance of the opera was to be on October 1st for a gala occasion in honour of Prince Anton of Saxony and the Archduchess Maria Theresa, a sister of Joseph II, who were coming through Prague on their honeymoon[3]. But as the opera had not been sufficiently rehearsed, Mozart directed *Figaro* instead, with the usual applause[4].

In the letter to von Jacquin already mentioned Mozart writes about this occasion: "You probably think that my opera is over by now. If so, you are a little mistaken. In the first place, the

---

[1] The recitative with these two passages is missing in the original score, which seems to confirm this anecdote told by Gugler.

[2] Prochazka, p. 86. The Prague libretto does not contain any of Leporello's comments on the pieces performed. His remark "They are musicians from Prague!" in Mozart's translation fragment also belongs to this category.

[3] The opera performed at their wedding on October 1st had been Martin's *Arbore di Diana*, which had nine performances in the same year. The libretto for the Prague performance of *Don Giovanni* had already been published in Vienna with the remark "Da rappresentarsi nel teatro di Praga per l'arrivo di S. A.R. Maria Teresa, Archiduchessa d'Austria, sposa del Ser. Principe Antonio di Sassonia, l'anno 1787". In it the first act finishes with the Quartet (No. 8); all the rest of the act is missing; the second act is complete.

[4] On October 13th Bondini, who had applied for permission to perform Beaumarchais' *Figaro*, was told by the Court that this piece would be allowed only as "an Italian opera, as performed at the Court theatre in Vienna" — not as a play.

stage personnel here are not as smart as those in Vienna, when it comes to mastering an opera of this kind in a very short time. Secondly, I found on my arrival that so few preparations and arrangements had been made that it would have been absolutely impossible to produce it on the 14th, that is, yesterday. So yesterday my *Figaro* was performed in a fully lighted theatre and I myself conducted. In this connexion I have a good joke to tell you. A few of the leading ladies here, and in particular one very high and mighty one, were kind enough to find it very ridiculous, unsuitable, and Heaven knows what else that the Princess should be entertained with a performance of *Figaro*, the "Crazy Day"[1], as the management were pleased to call it. It never occurred to them that no opera in the world, unless it is written specially, can be exactly suitable for such an occasion and that therefore it was of absolutely no consequence whether this or that opera were given, provided that it was a good opera and one which the Princess did not know: and *Figaro* at least fulfilled this last condition. In short by her persuasive tongue the ringleader brought things to such a pitch that the government forbade the impresario to produce this opera on that night. So she was triumphant! "Ho vinto", she called out one evening from her box. No doubt she never suspected that the *ho* might be changed to *sono*. But the following day Le Noble appeared, bearing a command from His Majesty to the effect that if the new opera could not be given, *Figaro* was to be performed! My friend, if only you had seen the handsome, magnificent nose of this lady! Oh, it would have amused you as much as it did me! *Don Giovanni* has now been fixed for the 24th.

"October 21st. It was fixed for the 24th, but a further postponement has been caused by the illness of one of the singers. As the company is so small, the impresario is in a perpetual state of anxiety and has to spare his people as much as possible, lest some unexpected indisposition should plunge him into the most awkward of all situations, that of not being able to produce any show whatsoever!

"So everything dawdles along here because the singers, who are lazy, refuse to rehearse on opera days and the manager, who is

---

[1] The sub-title of Beaumarchais' comedy *Le mariage de Figaro* is *La folle journée.*

anxious and timid, will not force them. . .

"October 25th. Today is the eleventh day that I have been scrawling this letter. You will see from this that my intentions are good. Whenever I can snatch a moment, I daub in another little piece. But indeed I cannot spend much time over it, because I am far too much at the disposal of other people and far too little at my own. I need hardly tell you, as we are such old friends, that this is not the kind of life I prefer.

"My opera is to be performed for the first time next Monday, October 29th. You shall have an account of it from me a day or two later. As for the aria, it is absolutely impossible to send it to you for reasons which I shall give you when we meet."[1]

No wonder that Mozart looked forward to the performance with some misgiving, since he was fully aware of the great difference between the new opera and *Figaro*. Only when the leader of the orchestra, J. B. Kucharz[2], calmed him down did his courage return, and he assured Kucharz that he had taken exceptional trouble for Prague.

There are conflicting opinions about when the overture was composed. To make the "miracle" complete, some assumed that it was the night before the first performance, which would mean that the orchestra played the overture at sight and Mozart earned special praise despite the many notes that "fell under the desk". Others, however, say it was finished two nights before the premiere; they include Konstanze, Mozart's wife, and this opinion is confirmed by Mozart's catalogue, in which the whole opera, including the Overture, is entered on October 28th. All this points to the night of 27th/28th, that is, the night before the final rehearsal. It would mean crediting the composer/conductor with

---

[1] This and the succeeding excerpt from Mozart's letters to G. von Jacquin are quoted in the translation from *Letters from Mozart and his family* by Emily Anderson, by permission of the publishers, Macmillan, London and Basingstoke.

[2] Kucharz (1751-1829), born in Chotecz, a pupil of Joseph Seegers, was first organist at the Heinrichskirche in Prague; in 1790 he was at the Stiftskirche in Strahow, and a conductor of the Prague Opera from 1791 to 1800. He was a respected virtuoso on the organ and wrote numerous works for the instrument, as well as dramatic music. He made the first vocal scores for *Figaro*, *Don Giovanni*, *Così fan tutte* and *Zauberflöte*; for the last he also wrote recitatives for performances in Prague in 1794.

excessive "courage" to suppose that on such an important occasion he would dare to let the orchestra play so difficult a piece from uncorrected parts.

The first performance was a brilliant success. *Die Ober-postamtzeitung* of November 3rd reports: "On Monday 29th the Italian opera company in Prague performed the eagerly-awaited opera by Maestro Mozart, *Don Giovanni*, or *The Stone Guest*. Connoisseurs and musicians say that nothing like it has ever been heard in Prague. Mr. Mozart himself conducted, and was greeted with repeated cheers as he came into the pit. The opera is, incidentally, extremely difficult, and everyone admired the fine performance after so short a rehearsal period. Theatre and orchestra did everything in their power for Mozart as a token of gratitude. A good deal of money had to be spent on the chorus and the decor, which was provided in excellent style by Mr. Guardasoni. The extraordinarily large audience was an indication of the general approval".[1]

The cast of this performance was as follows:

Don Giovanni	Sign. Luigi Bassi
Donna Anna	Sgra Teresa Saporiti
Don Ottavio	Sign. Antonio Baglioni
Commendatore	Sign. Giuseppe Lolli
Donna Elvira	Sra. Caterina Micelli
Leporello	Sign. Felice Ponziani
Masetto	Sign. Giuseppe Lolli
Zerlina	Sgra. Teresina(!) Bondini

Guardasoni[2] wrote enthusiastically to da Ponte, who had had to return to Vienna before the performance for rehearsals of Salieri's *Axur*: "Evviva da Ponte, evviva Mozart! Tutti gli impresarii, tutti i virtuosi devono benedirli! Finchè essi vivranno, non si saprà mai, cosa sia miseria teatrale". Mozart also reported the success to him at once and wrote to Gottfried von Jacquin on November 4th: "Dearest, most beloved friend, I hope you received my letter. My opera *Don Giovanni* had its first performance on

[1] Since the original programme no longer exists, this cast list has been put together from the Prague libretto and from the information obtained from Stiepanek. The first name of the Zerlina was Caterina, not Teresina.

[2] He was then Associate Director of the theatre with Bondini, and later sole Director. There was some adverse publicity about his passion for money and his lack of consideration for others.

October 29th and was received with the greatest applause. It was performed yesterday for the fourth time, for my benefit. I am thinking of leaving here on the 12th or 13th. When I return, you shall have the aria at once, remember, *between ourselves*. How I wish that my good friends, particularly you and Bridi, were here just for one evening in order to share my pleasure! But perhaps my opera will be performed in Vienna after all! I hope so. People here are doing their best to persuade me to stay on for a couple of months and write another one. But I cannot accept this proposal, however flattering it may be".

Luigi Bassi, the first Don Giovanni, was then 22 years old, having been born in Pesaro in 1765[1]. A pupil of Norandini in Sinigaglia and of Laschi in Florence, he was called a "fiery Italian" by Beethoven, while Meissner describes him as a "most beautiful but utterly stupid fellow". The register of the Bondini Company of which he had been a member since 1784 says in 1792: "His voice is as mellifluous as his acting is masterly. He is therefore applauded equally in comic and tragic parts, and pleases wherever he appears". He worked in Prague until 1806. Towards the end of the 1790s he began to lose the voice which a Prague report had thus described: "Its range is between tenor and bass, and although its sound is somewhat bright, it is always flexible, full and agreeable. Bassi is also a very skilful actor, who handles tragedy without being absurd, and comedy without lapses of taste. When he is in a mischievous mood he will, for instance, parody the faults of the other singers so exquisitely that only the audience, not the singers, are aware of it. His best roles are Axur, Teodoro (in Paisiello's *Re Teodoro*), the Notary in *Molinara* (by Paisiello) and the Count in *Figaro*. He never spoils a part and is the only real actor in the present Italian company."

The Leporello, a basso buffo named Felice Ponziani (the Prague Figaro), was also acclaimed both as singer and actor, and was particularly famous for his characterizations. His vocal evenness and fine enunciation were also praised. Before going to Prague he had been employed in Parma; from 1792 onwards he was in Venice.

Giuseppe Lolli, who played Masetto and the Commendatore,

---

[1] He played the part without a beard, as can be seen in pictures by Kinniger and Ramberg.

15

was also a good singer. He too had been in Parma and Venice (1780-81).

The excellent tenor Antonio Baglioni, Mozart's first Ottavio, was praised by da Ponte chiefly for his interpretative artistry and good taste; the register of 1792 says that the sound of his voice had such beauty, purity and expressiveness that few companies could boast a tenor of such accomplishments. Later he sang the title role in *La Clemenza di Tito*. He had appeared in Venice in 1786, where we find him again in 1793-4.

Among the female singers Teresa Saporiti, the 24-year-old Donna Anna, was famous for her vocal artistry and her beauty. Her likeness has been preserved on a medallion that was among the possessions of a Dr. Schebek. After her triumphs in Prague, she also appeared in Italy, in Venice, Parma and Bologna. She died in Milan on March 17th, 1869, at the age of 106.

While nothing is known about the first Elvira, Catarina Micelli, except that she was an excellent member of the Prague company, the Zerlina, Caterina Bondini, wife of the Director, was the acknowledged darling of the Prague public, both as a singer and an actress; when *Figaro* was performed for her benefit on December 14th, 1786, there was a veritable flood of poems in her praise.

Even if there is a certain local patriotism in these reports, they do seem to show that Mozart must have been well pleased with the original cast of his opera. After the performance he spent a few more weeks in Prague, enjoying universal respect and homage, weeks that remained a pleasant memory for his friends[1]. Some other compositions date from this period, particularly the scena "Bella mia fiamma" (K. 528) written on November 3rd for Josepha Duschek. Again he had been late in delivering it, so she locked him in a summer-house at Bertramka and declared that she would not release him until he had finished the aria. Mozart did set to work, but said that he would not give it to her unless she sang it correctly at sight[2]. This was no easy task, for in the Andante at the words

---

[1] According to contemporary reports Mozart, on his return to Bertramka from the old part of the city, would drink "another cup of black coffee" at the Steinitz coffee house. "Sometimes the place was already closed; so Mozart would knock at the window and the landlord would make the coffee himself, which had to be very strong. He would wear a blue tailcoat with gilt buttons, nankeen knee breeches and stockings with buckled shoes".

[2] Reported by Mozart's son in a Berlin music periodical.

"quest' affanno, questo passo e terribile per me" he had given the voice a melodic line with such unusual intervals, accompanied by equally unexpected harmonies, that it required an extremely experienced singer to negotiate the task without preparation. The aria is one of the most remarkable of its kind. Two lieder also date from November 6th: "Des kleinen Friedrichs Geburtstag" (Little Frederick's birthday), from Campe's *Children's Library*, and Hölty's "Traumbild" (Dream Image) K. 529 and 530.

Mozart's great success in Prague was probably the reason one of his Masses was performed on December 6th in St. Nicholas's Church. "Everyone agreed that he was also a complete master in this kind of music", wrote the *Oberpostamtzeitung*.

By mid-November Mozart had returned to Vienna. Gluck died on November 15th, 1787, and Mozart's success in Prague seems to have persuaded the Emperor to give him the post of Kammermusikus on December 7th, 1787, in order to keep him in Vienna.

However, the Vienna performance of *Don Giovanni* was still a long way off. In 1787 Salieri had written the opera *Tarare* for Paris on a text by Beaumarchais, who had again used the stage as an arena for political and philosophical argument. By order of the Emperor, Salieri engaged da Ponte to turn this text into an Italian opera libretto, *Axur, re d'Ormus*; he also made important changes in the music. On January 8th, 1788 this work was performed for the wedding of Archduke Franz and Princess Elisabeth, was repeated 29 times in the same year with more and more success, and soon found its way abroad, though in artistic value it fell far short of his *Danaides*.

So for the time being there was no room for *Don Giovanni*. The first four months of 1788 were filled mainly with occasional compositions, but also with some important works for piano, such as the so-called Coronation Concerto (K. 537) of February 24th, the Allegro and Andante (K. 533) of January 3rd and the Adagio in B minor (K. 540) of March 19th.

It was not until May 7th, 1788, that the performance took place at the Burgtheater, by order of Joseph II. Da Ponte received 100 and Mozart 225 florins. It was a failure and the critics did nothing more than record the fact that it had taken place. Da Ponte says that everyone except Mozart thought that a mistake had been made somewhere. So additions were made, a few arias were altered

—still without success. Only very gradually, after the work had been repeated several times in rapid succession, at Da Ponte's instigation, were the Viennese able to come to terms with this unusual masterpiece.[1]

The cast in Vienna was as follows:

Don Giovanni	Francesco Albertarelli[2]
Donna Anna	Aloisia Lange
Donna Elvira	Caterina Cavalieri
Don Ottavio	Francesco Morella
Leporello	Francesco Benucci
Don Pedro	Francesco Bussani
Masetto	Francesco Bussani
Zerlina	Luisa Mombelli

According to his thematic catalogue, Mozart made the most important additions well before the performance; they are also found in the Vienna libretto. Dramatically they are all harmful. First there is Elvira's aria, "Mi tradì quell' alma ingrata", a concession to Signora Cavalieri;[3] secondly, the G major aria "Dalla sua pace" for the tenor Morella;[4] thirdly, a buffo duet between Zerlina and Leporello, "Per queste tue manine", a coarse little piece that is hardly connected with the story, completely out of character and calculated only to satisfy the public's desire for a good laugh.[5]

---

[1] *Don Giovanni* was performed 15 times that year, on 7, 9, 12, 16, 23, 30 May; 16, 23 June; 5, 11, 21 July; 2 August; 24, 31 October; 15 December. The statement in Lange's autobiography that the opera was put on the shelf after 3 performances is therefore incorrect. But after 1788 the work was kept ʻout of the theatre. It was not performed again until November 15, 1792, at the Theater auf der Wieden in a miserable German version by Spiess; on December 16, 1798 it was played in German at the Hoftheater nächst der Burg. According to da Ponte, the Emperor on hearing *Don Giovanni* said: "The opera is divine, perhaps even more beautiful than *Figaro*, but it is no food for the teeth of my Viennese". When Mozart heard this he replied: "Let us give them time to chew!" Joseph II moved to his Headquarters on February 28, 1788, and did not return to Vienna until December 5; he can therefore not have seen the opera before December 15.

[2] Not Mandini, as Freissauff repeatedly asserts.

[3] She wanted to sing it in D instead of E flat, which Mozart also had to concede.

[4] He had appeared at Easter, 1788, in Paisiello's *Barbiere*.

[5] The autograph of this piece is not extant, neither are its secco recitatives complete. Gugler doubted its authenticity.

Mozart himself made these alterations half-heartedly; they did not really help his opera much. The Viennese musicians and connoisseurs criticized the work a great deal, as we know; Haydn was the only one who supported Mozart without reservation.

Like *Figaro, Don Giovanni* was slow to gain a foothold on the German stage compared with the fashionable operas of the day. The first performance after the one in Vienna took place in Leipzig on June 15th, 1788, under the direction of Guardasoni, with members of the original Prague cast. In 1789 there came Mainz (May 23rd), Mannheim (September 27th, greatly applauded), Bonn (October 13th: "The music pleased the experts greatly; the action did not"), Frankfurt-am-Main and Hamburg (October 27th). Schink, who has some harsh words to say about the text, is all the more enthusiastic about the music: "Is this splendid, majestic and vigorous music really the stuff for ordinary opera-goers, who take their ears to the theatre but leave their hearts at home?

"What is beautiful, grand and noble in the *Don Giovanni* score will everywhere be obvious to a minority of chosen people. It is not music to everybody's taste, tickling the ear and starving the heart — Mozart is no ordinary composer. He does not provide light, pleasant little tunes at random. His music is thoughtful and deeply felt, appropriate to the personalities, situations and feelings of his characters. It is a study of language musically treated. He never encumbers his vocal line with unnecessary, soulless coloratura. This would banish true expression from music; expression is not confined to single words but arises from intelligent, natural unification of sounds which convey true feeling. This kind of expression Mozart has entirely in his power. Every note is felt and transformed into feeling. His expressiveness is glowing, lively and picturesque, without becoming excessive or self-indulgent. His imagination is at the same time both rich and controlled. He is the true virtuoso, whose inventiveness never runs away with his intellect; reasoning guides his enthusiasm, calm examination his creative powers".

There was also another Austrian performance in December, 1789, in Brno, which could not, however, rival Dittersdorf's *Figaro*. In 1790 there were performances in Budapest (date

19

uncertain), Soest (June 26th) and in Berlin[1] (December 20th, in the presence of the King). The success of the Berlin performance was quite exceptional,[2] but the critics' reaction was in part cold. The *Chronik von Berlin* said: "If ever an opera has been awaited with eagerness, if ever a work of Mozart's has been exalted to the skies before it was heard, it was *Don Giovanni*! That Mozart is an outstanding, even a great composer, the whole world will admit; but that nothing greater than this opera has ever been written or ever will be — that we beg leave to doubt. Theatrical music knows no other rule, no other judge than the heart; that is the only criterion of its value. It is not excessive instrumentation that counts. The heart, feelings and passions are what the composer must articulate; then he will write something great, then his name will go down to posterity. Grétry, Monsigny and Philidor will prove this. In *Don Giovanni* Mozart wanted to write something extraordinary, something inimitably great; certainly there is something extraordinary there, but nothing inimitably great! Whim, mood, pride, not the heart, created *Don Giovanni*, and we would rather be asked to admire the sublime possibilities in an oratorio or some other solemn church music of his than in this work".

Another critic praises the music (as was the rule in those early years) but criticizes the text all the more. He finds that the piece satisfies the eye and enchants the ear, but offends reason, outrages morality and allows vice to trample virtue and sensibility underfoot. "If ever a nation could be proud of one of its contemporaries, Germany can be of Mozart, the composer of this work. Never, surely, was the greatness of a man's mind more manifest; never did music reach a higher level! Melodies which an angel might have imagined are here accompanied by heavenly harmonies, and anyone whose soul is the least susceptible to the truly beautiful will, I am sure, forgive me if I say: 'The ear is spellbound'. But he cannot refrain from a pious wish: 'O that you had not wasted your spirit in this way! That your feeling had matched your imagination, and that the latter had not led you by such sordid paths to

---

[1] A Berlin report in the *Journal des Modes* says: "The composition of this Singspiel is fine, but here and there very artificial and instrumentally overloaded".

[2] The opera had five performances in ten days.

20

greatness! What can it profit you if your name be inscribed in diamond letters on a golden tablet — if the tablet is hung on a pillory!' "

Spazier, who acknowledged the "true, original and natural wealth of ideas in Mozart", and who said of *Don Giovanni* that some of its arias had more intrinsic value than whole operas by Paisiello, remarked on another occasion: "The delight we feel when an artistic genius follows an unusual course with ease, a course that would, we know very well, require immense effort from anyone else, can only be recaptured afterwards through intense study, especially when the artist strains his entire soul — as can be said of Mozart in *Don Giovanni*, where he overwhelms the listener with so many proofs of his art that the excellence of the whole is almost overlooked". Spazier did not carry out his promise to discuss the work in detail.

B.A. Weber, who had been in Berlin for a short time, was also sincere in admiring *Don Giovanni*: "If one unites a profound knowledge of the art with the most felicitous talent for inventing charming melodies, and then combines the two with the greatest possible originality, one can obtain a true picture of Mozart's musical genius. None of the ideas in his works are familiar, and even his accompaniments are always new. One is borne along without a moment's rest from one idea to the next, so that admiration for the last heard effaces the impression of what has gone before, and even exerting every possible effort, one can scarcely take in all the beauty. If one wished to find fault with Mozart, it would be that this abundance of excellence almost tires the mind, so that the effect of the whole is occasionally obscured. But hail to the artist whose only fault consists in too much perfection."[1] Since it is almost impossible, he adds, to go into the detail of a Mozart opera, because one cannot find a beginning or an end, he singles out what he considers the finest pieces, above all the Overture, then the Quartet, the first Finale, the Sextet and the

---

[1] Dittersdorf expressed the same opinion about Mozart to Joseph II: "He is undoubtedly one of the greatest original geniuses, and I have never known a composer with such an astonishing wealth of ideas. I wish he had not been so lavish with them. He allows the listener no breathing space; for no sooner does one stop to reflect on a beautiful theme than another splendid one arrives, displacing the previous one, and so it goes on; in the end one can remember none of these beautiful episodes".

conclusion of the opera, in which, he says, the horror of the scene is conveyed with such realism that one's hair actually stands on end; then to prove that Mozart also excels in cheerful scenes, he mentions the peasants' chorus and the entrancing duet "Là ci darem la mano", with its beguiling melody. He was, however, severely taken to task on this issue by a reader of the paper given to delivering himself of frank opinions: "His judgement of Mozart is highly exaggerated and one-sided. Nobody will deny that Mozart is talented and experienced, a resourceful and agreeable composer. All the same, I never found a real connoisseur of music who considered him to be a correct, much less a perfect artist; even less will a critic of taste see him as a composer who handles poetry with skill and finesse".

The *Musikzeitung* (1793) wrote as follows: "Mozart was a great genius; however, he actually had little culture and little or no informed taste. In his otherwise original works for the theatre he occasionally missed the effect, the main point of interest in opera; and as for proper treatment of words, can anyone maintain that he (Mozart) knew how to handle a text properly or that his music is ever one with the poetry?"

These differing views give a more or less complete picture of critical reaction: both praise and blame show that on all sides there was recognition that here was a work of the greatest significance.[1]

In 1791 there were more performances, in Hanover, Kassel (April 16th) and in Munich (August 7th), where the opera came under the Censor's ban which was later lifted on orders from the highest authority. In 1792 came Breslau (January 20th), Glogau (July 26th) and Weimar (January 30th), where it had only a moderate success like *Figaro* in 1793: here too only the performances of *Zauberflöte* in 1794 opened the way for its two predecessors, and on 30th December, 1797 Goethe wrote to Schiller: "The hopes you had for opera you might have seen fulfilled to a high degree quite recently in *Don Giovanni*; however, this work stands entirely on its own, and Mozart's death has destroyed any prospect of its being repeated".

---

[1] All the same, Jacob wrote to Herder (July, 1792): "We were extremely bored at the opera yesterday; what an unbearable thing, this *Don Giovanni*. A good thing that it is now behind us."

On October 24th came Bremen, and in 1793 the court theatres of Braunschweig, Passau and Münster; J. Böhm performed the work with his company in Düsseldorf, Cologne and Aachen, as did Schuch in Konigsberg and the following year in Danzig. In 1794 it was put on in Oels and Schleswig, and in 1795 in Kiel, Magdeburg and Nürnberg. The last town of importance was Stuttgart, where *Don Giovanni* was given on March 28th, 1796, in a highly burlesque presentation.

Public recognition was now general; soon there was no German theatre where *Don Giovanni* was not a permanent feature. In Vienna, according to Sonnenleiter, it had been given 531 times by the end of 1863; in Prague, according to Stiepanek, the opera had 116 performances in the first ten years, and 360 by 1863; in Berlin it had been given more than 200 times before the 50th jubilee performance in 1837, an occasion also marked solemnly in Prague and Magdeburg.[1] The centenary on October 29th, 1887, was celebrated all over Germany as a homage to Mozart's memory. The Berlin centenary performance was the 497th, the two, in Prague (in Italian and German) the 534th and 535th. Vienna presented a new translation by Kalbeck.

In Paris, the work was first heard in 1805, in a dreadfully distorted and mutilated version by C. Kalbrenner. One example will suffice: the masked Terzetto was sung by three gendarmes to the words "Courage, vigilance, Adresse, défiance, Que l'active prudence Préside à nos desseins". Music by Kalkbrenner was also inserted, but all the same this concoction found favour with the public for some time. In 1811 *Don Giovanni* was first performed by the opera company at the Théâtre Italien where it has continued ever since. Finally a new French version was provided by Castil-Blaze, who had already made one attempt in 1822 at Lyon, and another in 1827 at the Odéon in Paris. In 1834 the opera was brilliantly presented at the Académie de Musique with an excellent cast, in a version more faithful to the original. A newly-edited version was given in 1866 at the Théâtre Lyrique under the direction of Carvalho.

In London the great success of *Figaro* paved the way for *Don Giovanni*; on April 12th, 1817, it was given at the King's Theatre

---

[1] By May, 1890 the Royal Opera in Berlin had given 523 performances. On June 12th, 1902, the 600th was celebrated with a gala presentation.

for the first time, and has ever since been regarded as one of the finest achievements of Italian opera. The applause for the first performance in Italian was so great that the proprietor of Covent Garden authorized an English version, which was presented with some success on May 20th of the same year in a fine performance.[1]

Though *Don Giovanni* found a home in the North, being presented also in Amsterdam (1794), Reval (1797), Copenhagen (1807) and Stockholm (1813), it did not manage to gain ground with the Italian public, despite repeated attempts, although a number of connoisseurs showed appreciation. Florence came first in 1792 — we know nothing about its reception. In 1817 and 1818, when the opera was given in a mutilated version, it met with no success. But later (1834), when presented in its original form, it was received with great applause.[2] In 1811 it was given in Rome, well rehearsed in the original score, and won a succès d'estime. It was decided that it was "una musica bellissima, superba, sublime, un musicone", but not really "de gusto del paese"; the many stranezze might well be very lovely, but people were just not used to them.[3] In Naples (1812) the result was similar. In both cases the success was short-lived. In Milan (1814) there was as much whistling as clapping, but later performances found more favour. In Turin the opera is said to have pleased, though it was badly performed. In 1818 it was put on in Bologna, and in 1821 in Parma with mediocre results. In Genoa it pleased the connoisseurs but not the general public, and in Venice (1833) it won only modest approval in the course of time. The comment of one lady singer is typical: "Non capisco niente a questa musica maledetta!" Against this, however, one can put Rossini's answer, when asked which of his own operas he preferred: "Vous voulez connaître celui de mes ouvrages que j'aime le mieux: eh bien, c'est *Don Giovanni*".[4] In Spain *Don Giovanni* was first shown in Madrid in 1834.

[1] According to the *Musical Times* of 1887 it was entitled *The Libertine*, translation by Pocock, the music edited by Sir H. R. Bishop.

[2] In 1857 the "outmoded, hyperborean music" was whistled off the stage there so thoroughly that the second performance was cancelled.

[3] Stendhal, *Vie de Rossini*.

[4] Rossini gave this answer after his arrival in Paris (1823), where his style was frequently used as an argument against Mozart.

Nine years earlier, in 1825, da Ponte had prevailed upon Garcia, who was giving Italian opera in New York, to present *Don Giovanni* there. In spite of dreadful mishaps,[1] the opera had a warm reception, and da Ponte, who invested his large income from his libretti in lottery tickets, made a considerable profit.

---

[1] In the first Finale there was such complete chaos that Garcia, who was an excellent Don Giovanni, finally called for silence, sword in hand, and shouted that a masterpiece should not be ruined in this way. They began again and brought the Finale to a successful end. A friend of da Ponte's who regularly slept through operatic performances assured him that such an opera would even prevent him from sleeping for the rest of the night!

DON GIOVANNI

It is a tribute to da Ponte's understanding of Mozart's personality that he should have suggested the subject of *Don Giovanni* to him. Don Juan has featured prominently in poetry everywhere for at least three centuries, proving that his problems, like those of Faust, relate to the fundamental questions of human existence. While Faust represents a yearning for a higher meaning in life, a striving for salvation, Don Juan's world is that of the senses, recognizing no other values than its own. He knows nothing of Faust's 'striving toil', but only the 'to be or not to be' of Renaissance man; and it is therefore no coincidence that the subject was first treated dramatically in the Catholic south of Europe, where the medieval doctrine of the sinfulness of all flesh has never been wholly accepted.

No historical foundation for the story has yet been established. Tradition and legend seem to have provided most of the material; on the one hand the figure, already familiar in the Middle Ages and becoming more significant in the Renaissance, of the unbridled man of the senses, and on the other the ancient myth of the dead man who returns as a statue to avenge a misdeed. The two themes appear together for the first time in *El Burlador de Sevilla, y convidada de pietra*, printed in 1630, by Tirso de Molina — the pseudonym of Gabriel Tellez, a monk and prior whose authorship, however, has recently been strongly contested.[1] This comedy, with all its poetic felicities of detail, is a strangely hybrid work. Don Juan, it is true, grows beyond the role of a merely ruthless villain; even in crime he shows real stature and is chivalrous as well as fearless. Nor does he lack truly human features, as is shown by his inner hesitation before the fateful supper in the graveyard chapel. Only when the end is inevitable does his strength desert him, and he asks for a priest in a vain attempt to repent. Here the underlying character of the piece

---

[1] Particularly by Farinelli. On the basis of the second version of the piece, entitled 'Tan largo me lo fiais?' Schröder even tried to ascribe the authorship to Calderon.

26

emerges clearly, as it also does in the figure of the Commendatore (here called Don Gonzalo de Ulloa), who not only appears as the avenger of a wrong done to himself, but also as the personification of human morality.

Don Juan's servant Catalinon is the favourite (*gracioso*) of the piece, loyal and devoted to his master, yet by no means approving his actions. His comedy is much more reticent than the later Leporello's, and in particular his cowardly nature is not yet as apparent as it later becomes.

As regards the female characters, the first thing to be said is that Don Juan's only concern with them is to satisfy his masculine egotism. The demoniac quality of the sensual man is still entirely absent; he behaves quite unscrupulously, simply delighting in seduction. But one cannot speak of passion or of love with the women, either; they are won over partly by deceit, partly by promises of marriage. Donna Anna hardly asserts herself, and the passionate Tisbea shows only a few characteristics of Elvira, whereas in the rustic couple Aminta and Patricio the characters of Zerlina and Masetto are already recognizable. All these minor characters are only loosely connected with the main plot, like the Duchess Isabella, who also in some ways resembles Elvira. The Marquis de la Mota, Donna Anna's fiancé, eventually becomes Duke Octavio; he finally wins the hand of Isabella, originally intended for Don Juan.

The action already contains the main features of the later libretto: the murder of the Commendatore, the rustic wedding with the seduction of the bride, the inscription on the tombstone and finally the invitation and then the appearance of the statue; except that after the meal at Don Juan's house, the Commendatore asks him to another in his mausoleum, where he is served with scorpions, snakes, vinegar and gall, to the accompaniment, not of *Tafelmusik*, but of a chant calling him to repent. Then follows retribution, after which the whole piece closes with Catalinon's account of his master's end and the wedding of the two couples.

From Spain the story travelled next to Naples, with the publication in 1652 of *Convitato da pietra, rappresentazione in prosa* by Onofrio Giliberti. The text has been lost, and so we are left wholly in the dark about its relationship with the *Burlador* or any later works. We do not even know if the piece of the same title by

Andrea Cicognini was written earlier or not (it appeared in print in 1671, some twenty years after Cicognini's death). Both pieces were obviously real *commedie dell'arte* and distorted the story in a burlesque fashion. The original course of the action was only roughly followed; anything at all sublime or religious was cut out, and the main interest was concentrated on Arlecchino, the hero's servant, and his jokes. There was a new treatment of the story by Andrea Perrucci (1678), but this has also disappeared.[1]

Whether the two French verse dramas both entitled 'Le Festin de pierre ou le fils criminel' by Dorimond (1658) and de Villiers (1659) are connected with Giliberti is open to question, although de Villiers talks of a translation from the Italian. In any case, they are offshoots of the Italian *commedia dell'arte* idea and none too refined at that; as before, the frivolous pranks of the master and particularly of the servant are the main subject.[2]

On February 15, 1665, the Théâtre du Palais Royal gave the first performance of *Dom Juan ou Le festin de Pierre* by Molière (first printed in the Oeuvres of 1682), the poet's first comedy in prose. Molière probably knew the *Burlador* and certainly the Italian farce as well as its two French derivatives, but these models cannot compare in vitality with his own. Molière was a genuine child of Louis XIV's time and so the essence of his hero is not sensuality but rationalism. He is a typical cavalier of the age: fearless and a perfect master of all courtly etiquette, but also a cold, and above all, egotistical creature of reason, without sensuality, passion or heart. It is significant that he not only blasphemes like his predecessors but even denies the existence of God. Piety to him is mere hypocrisy and a useful weapon in achieving his own ends. As a result, his invitation to the statue naturally loses much of its dramatic force; it has the effect of a cynical game, not of a challenge to the divine power by a man whose demoniacal impulses know no bounds.

All in all, what is the purpose of so many fantastic and roman-

[1] The character of this 'opera tragica in prosa' remains obscure. The very description makes it doubtful whether it can have been an opera.
[2] The figure of the Hermit, also found in Molière's character 'Le Pauvre' and in some German folk plays, is new. Even in Mozart's opera this scene was inserted for a long time, for instance by Schikaneder in his Vienna performance of 1792. Also new is the relationship of the hero to his father, Don Alvaro.

tic, in short, irrational features in this rationalistic, tendentious drama? The confrontation with the supernatural in the shape of the veiled woman, who at the end pronounces judgement on the hero and then suddenly turns herself into an allegory of Time with a scythe is typically French. Molière's treatment adds psychological depth to the subject for the first time since the *Burlador*; on the other hand, he found himself, in the new character drama that he had created, in insoluble conflict with the essential elements of the story itself.

The character of Don Juan's servant Sganarelle, who resembles the Italian Arlecchino, is developed in so far as Molière wanted to make him a contrast to his hero. For Sganarelle reasons as morally as Don Juan does immorally, and is the same kind of egotist, only a cowardly one.[1] Of the women, Donna Anna pales considerably: both her seduction and the murder of her father are merely reported in passing. On the other hand, the character of Donna Elvira is essentially Molière's creation beside which all previous attempts seem colourless. Don Juan entices her from a nunnery and marries her, only to desert her soon afterwards. She follows him, but in doing so discovers his true nature and decides to return to the convent. First, however, she visits him once more, not to reproach him but to induce him to change his ways and to save him from disaster. This noble renunciation of love bears the mark of the great dramatist, though it does not redeem other fundamental faults in the work. Elvira's two brothers, Don Carlos and Don Alonso, stand by her to avenge her honour, but fail to achieve their end.

That the fierce satire was immediately appreciated is proved by the fact that the play only had fifteen performances, and was not published in Molière's lifetime. Only the adaptation in Alexandrian verse by Thomas Corneille (1677) was staged: it eliminated the most offensive passages, including the final pages.[2] The last French *Don Juan*, Rosimond's *Nouveau festin de Pierre ou l'Athée*

---

[1] His cry of grief at Don Juan's death, 'Mes gages! Mes gages!' caused much offence at the first performance.

[2] The original version did not appear again until 1841 at the Odéon and 1847 at the Théâtre Français.

foudroyé is poetically quite unoriginal and worthless.[1]

The rest of Europe was at first indebted to these French authors, particularly Molière. In 1676 Thomas Shadwell's 'The Libertine', based on Molière and Rosimond, was performed in London. It had a great success, but the general impression was so terrifying 'as to render it little less than impiety to represent it on the stage'.[2] In Holland too, there were several plays showing the French influence, by Adrian Reys (1699), van Maaler (1719) and others. At the same time (1690) Johannes Velten produced a German translation in Torgau under the title *Don Juan oder Don Pedros Totengastmahl.*

After this the story soon established itself in Germany and became particularly popular with improvising companies of actors. Thus the famous clown Gottfried Prehauser took the role of Don Philippo in *The Stone Guest*; it was his first dramatic appearance in Vienna.[3] Until 1772 there were also regular performances of a *Don Juan, or The Stone Guest* in Vienna on All Souls' Day. The nature of the two plays is unfortunately no longer known. One might reasonably imagine Prehauser's to have been one of the popular burlesque impromptu comedies that were then the fashion in Vienna. The play *Schrecken im Spiegel des ruchlosen Jugend, oder das Lehrreiche Gastmahl des Don Pedro,*[4] was probably in a similar vein. In 1752 the Royal Polish and Electoral Saxon Court Comedians performed a piece in Dresden with the truly rationalistic title of *Das steinerne Totengastmahl, oder die im Grab noch lebende Rache, oder die aufs höchste gestiegene, enlich übel angekommene Kühn— und Freichheit.*[5] In 1766 Schröder

---

[1] Its action is cautiously laid in heathen times, so as to allow the 'atheist' to brag with impunity.

[2] Erskine Baker : *Biographia Dramatica*, London 1782.

[3] This Don Philippo also appears in the works of Dorimond and de Villiers, but as a serious character, corresponding to the later Don Ottavio. As a result, conclusions have been drawn as to the origins of the lost Viennese play. Could Prehauser have played such a serious role? Might not the comic Viennese character of Lipperl be hidden behind the grand name?

[4] *The Terror in the Mirror of Reckless Youth, or the Instructive Banquet of Don Pedro.*

[5] *The Stone Banquet of the Dead, or Vengeance still living in the Grave, or Extreme Boldness and Impudence finally come to grief.*

triumphed in Hamburg as Sganarelle, which suggests a version of Molière. Of the 18th century folk plays we have only the so-called *Laufner Don Juan* which treats the legend in a fairly coarse manner, claiming the authorship of Metastasio merely in order to attract the public.

The numerous puppet plays performed around the same time in Augsburg, Ulm, Strasbourg and other towns are works of the same type. Titles like *Don Juan, or the Quadruple Murderer, or the Midnight Banquet in the Cemetery* speak for themselves. Of course the clown is the main character. The connexion with the earlier French pieces is clear, particularly with regard to the Hermit scene which appears frequently; but whether any direct use was made of Dorimond and de Villiers is doubtful. The last of these folk plays about Don Juan is the comedy *Don Juan or the Stone Guest*, adapted from Molière and the Spanish of Tirso de Molina, adding Kaspar's *Amusements*, which Karl Marinelli, the Director of the Leopoldstädter Theater in Vienna, put on 81 times between 1783 and 1821. In Spain a new version appeared in 1725 under the title *No hay plazo que no se cumpla ni deuda que no se pague, y convidado de piedra*[1] by Antonio de Zamora, a pretty loosely fashioned piece which presents the hero as a common theatrical villain and could have been of no interest to da Ponte.

In Italy too, the story enjoyed lasting popularity in the form of a farce. No less a man than Goldoni decided to replace what he considered the bad Italian and French versions by something better. In his *Don Giovanni Tenorio ossia ill Dissoluto*, performed in Venice (1736), he achieved this in a thoroughly rationalistic way, like Molière, but not with the same success; in other words, he made it a comedy about sensible, practical life, in which there is no room for passion or miracles. Thus in the end the hero is simply struck by lightning, and the invitation of the statue is missing completely; coarse burlesque is excluded, but so is profundity. In the coquettish character of Elisa, a feeble attempt at a Zerlina figure, Goldoni also wanted to take personal vengeance on the actress Passalacqua who had jilted him — in short, the play is one of his weakest works. All the same, thanks to his prestige, it provided several features for later libretti. Thus Isabella (Elvira) is

---

[1] *There is Neither Time Unaccomplished nor Debt Unpaid, or The Stone Guest.*

declared insane by Don Giovanni before the first challenge to a duel. Donna Anna is also promised to Don Ottavio without much affection and at times feels definite sympathy for Don Giovanni; while Don Ottavio is already the wavering, passive character known to us from da Ponte's libretto. The subtitle of the latter, *Il Dissoluto*, is also derived from Goldoni.

Meanwhile the story had reached the operatic stage. In 1713 the Théâtre de la Foire in Paris presented the three-act *Le Festin de Pierre, en vaudeville sans prose*; it was evidently one of those vaudeville comedies with music which Le Sage loved to perform. The composer was Le Tellier. Despite public enthusiasm the piece was at first banned because of the representation of Hell in the final scene; but eventually it was permitted. The treatment of the story was entirely in the humorous style of the earlier opéra comique composers. In Italy Don Giovanni first appears in 1734, in an opera called *La pravità castigata* played by A. Mingotti's company[1]. The composer was Eustacchio Bambini; the libretto was very loosely put together in the spirit of the popular impromptu farce, and it relied a good deal on vulgar machine effects on the stage. In 1746 Colin Restier presented a ballet *Le grand Festin de Pierre* — of which only the title remains — at the Théâtre de la Foire Laurent.

But the ballet *Don Juan*, performed at the Vienna Kärntnertortheater in 1761, has been completely preserved. It is by Gasparo Angiolini, the then director of the ballet, with music by Gluck. (Criticism of the idea of treating the subject in ballet form disappeared thanks to the influence of Noverre and his circle.) Angiolini describes his *Don Juan* as a 'Ballet Pantomime dans le goût des anciens' and demands simplicity and grandeur in the characters and in the action, which is constructed with the utmost economy. Of the women only Donna Anna appears at all, as the mistress of Don Juan and the niece of the Komthur. The first part includes Don Juan's serenade in front of Donna Anna's house and the murder of the Komthur; the second, Don Juan's banquet with the appearance of the statue — who invites him back; the third, the Komthur's attempts to convert Don Juan; the fourth his torture by the Furies and his final destruction in the fires of Hell. This version certainly simplifies the action to the utmost, but it

---

[1] There is no proof that Mingotti was the librettist.

also leaves out essential characteristics of the hero and reduces Donna Anna to the role of being a slave to his will. Thanks to Gluck's music the work soon travelled abroad, to Paris and especially to Italy, where it was put on in Parma, Turin, Naples and Milan. Another *Don Juan* ballet, most probably by Fr. L. Schröder, was performed by Ackermann's company in 1769.

In the seventies the Italian theatres were positively flooded with 'convitati di pietra', a sure sign of the popularity which the subject enjoyed. First came the *Dramma tragicomico*, set to a text of Filistri by V. Righini, which also appeared in Prague (1776) and in Vienna (1777). It begins, following older models, with Don Giovanni and his servant Arlecchino being saved from drowning by a couple of fishermen. Then follows Don Giovanni's assault on the honour of Donna Anna (here compulsorily married to the Duca Ottavio) and the murder of the Commendatore, after which Donna Anna swears vengeance on the murderer. Don Giovanni decides to flee, but is pursued by Isabella, whom he has seduced, and who urges Don Alfonso to punish him. After a vain attempt to change Donna Anna's mind, Don Giovanni makes Arlecchino invite the Statue. The meal takes its course with Don Giovanni toasting the public and Arlecchino the pretty girls; then the Statue appears and invites Don Giovanni. At the meeting in the mausoleum his fate is sealed. Anna and Alfonso are told what has happened; Don Giovanni is plagued by the Furies in Hell.

This libretto mixes serious and buffo elements in a colourful way. Of another 'convitato di pietra', performed in Venice (1777) with music by Giuseppe Calegari, only the title remains, and the same is true of the work by Giochino Albertini (Venice, 1784). On the other hand, the poet G.B. Lorenzi, in his libretto for Giacomo Tritto (Naples, 1783), reverted to the old version by Cicognini and gave the character of Pulcinella an important role.

But it was in 1787 that Italian enthusiasm for the Don Juan story reached its peak. Goethe told his friend Zelter as late as 1815 that he remembered the time when, in Rome, 'an opera called *Don Juan* (not Mozart's) was played every night for four weeks, which excited the city so much that the lowliest grocers' families were to be found in the stalls and boxes with their children and other relations, and no one could bear to live without having fried Don Juan in Hell, or seen the Commendatore, as a

33

blessed spirit, ascend to heaven.'[1] To which work these words refer cannot be established with certainty; for in the autumn of 1787 the Teatro della Valle presented a one-act farce entitled *Il convitato di pietra* (after Lorenzi) with music by Vincenzo Fabrizi. Moreover, a *Nuovo convitato die pietra* is known to have been performed in Venice during the carnival season of the same year. Its librettist has been forgotten, but the composer was Francesco Gardi; the text is again a fairly rough and ready farce. The addition of the word 'nuovo', however, implies that a well-known work of the same name already existed, and this was most probably the *Convitato di pietra* by Guiseppe Bertati and Giovanni Gazzaniga, the most successful version of all, which had been performed in January 1787 at the Teatro San Moisè in Venice.

Its predecessor was a 'capriccio drammatico', an adaptation of Bertati's Prologue, *La Novità* of 1775. In this prologue the opera director Policastro tells his company that in order to please the German public he wishes to present something new, namely, the one-act comedy of the Stone Guest. A noble patron of the theatre tries to dissuade the players from this plan, and actually they all want to stop rehearsing. The Impresario threatens not to pay their salaries, and the rehearsal takes place, accompanied by all kinds of jokes. The Prologue is followed by a second act, this being the *Convitato di pietra* of which Bertati is almost certainly the author, though this is not definitely stated. Evidently the Prologue represents one of those parodies on the running of a theatre that were particularly popular in opera buffa. Its music, apart from a few additions by Giovanni Valentini, was that of the *Stone Guest* by Gazzaniga.[2] The work soon became known all over Italy, in Varese, Bologna, Ferrara, Bergamo, Milan and Lucca. In 1791 the opera was played in Paris with Cherubini contributing an additional quartet; in 1792 it was heard in Lisbon and finally, in 1794, in London, even though da Ponte, who was present, objected to the numerous additions, which included Mozart's own catalogue aria.[3] Much of the full score of the opera still exists in several

---

[1] Oddly enough in his *Italian Journey* not a word of this is mentioned.

[2] For more detail see F. Chrysander: *The Don Giovanni Operas by Gazzaniga and Mozart*, where part of the text of the Prologue can be found together with the entire text of the opera, and a few bars of Gazzaniga's music.

[3] Da Ponte : *Memoirs* Vol. II.

incomplete copies which partly supplement one another — but the libretto is preserved intact. The Dramatis Personae are:

D. Giovanni

D. Anna figlia del Commendatore d'Oljola

D. Elvira Sposa promessa di D. Giovanni

D. Ximena Dama di Villena

Il Commendatore Padre di D. Anna

Duca Ottavio Sposo promesso della medesima

Maturina Sposa promessa di Biagio

Pasquariello Servo confidente di D. Giovanni

Biagio Contadino sposo di Maturina

Lanterna altro Servo di D. Giovanni

Servitori diversi, che non parlano

La Scene è in Villena nell'Aragona

The singer playing Donna Anna also sang the part of Maturina while the Commendatore also sang Biagio. The action was as follows:

Pasquariello, in a bad mood, is keeping watch outside the house of the Commendatore when Don Giovanni dashes out, struggling to disengage himself from Donna Anna who is trying to tear off his mask while calling her father to the rescue. He appears, and falls in the ensuing duel. The first scene closes with a trio for the men. (There is no overture). After a short conversation Don Giovanni runs away with Pasquariello. Donna Anna enters hurriedly with her fiancé Don Ottavio and finds, to her horror, the body of her father (accompanied recitative); more composed, she recounts in detail Don Giovanni's attack and declares that she will retire to a convent until Ottavio has discovered and punished the murderer (aria), to which Ottavio, with much grief, consents (aria). (Donna Anna does not appear again.) Don Giovanni, waiting for Donna Ximena in a country house, is talking to Pasquariello when Donna Elvira enters in travelling attire, having followed him from Burgos where he abandoned her (aria). When they recognize each other Don Giovanni refers her to Pasquariello as to the reasons for his departure and absconds. Pasquariello shows her the catalogue of his employer's mistresses (aria); she determines to obtain justice or take vengeance. Don Giovanni arrives in amorous conversation with Ximena and, in answer to her jealous enquiries, assures her of his good faith (aria). A rustic bride and bridegroom, Maturina and Biagio, are celebrating their wedding (Chorus and Tarantella). Pasquariello, mingling with the country folk, pays court to the bride but has to retreat when Don Giovanni joins the company and treats the bridegroom so roughly that he goes away in a temper (aria). Through flattery and promise of marriage Don Giovanni deceives Maturina, who also assures him of her love (aria). Ximena asks Pasquariello for information about his master and is very pleased when he reassures her about Don Giovanni's fidelity. Don Giovanni joins them and is questioned in turn by Ximena, Elvira and Maturina, managing to pacify each one by telling her that the other two are madly infatuated with him.[1] (Duet in which Elvira and Maturina quarrel after the others have left). In the mausoleum built by the Commendatore during his lifetime, Duca Ottavio has an inscription placed at the foot of the statue. Don Giovanni comes to look at the monument with Pasquariello and forces him to invite the statue to supper (duet). In Don Giovanni's house, Lanterna the cook prepares the meal and awaits his master; Elvira arrives and, when Don Giovanni comes home with Pasquariello, implores him to repent; he rejects the idea with scorn and Elvira leaves him, to go to a convent (aria). Don Giovanni sits down cheerfully to dinner to the sound of *Tafelmusik* (concertino); Pasquariello has to sit with him, while Lanterna does the serving; they toast the city of Venice and its beautiful ladies (Pasquariello's aria).[2] There is a knock at the door, and to the horror of the two servants the Commendatore appears. Don Giovanni bids him welcome and orders Pasquariello

---

[1] The quartet 'Non ti fidar o misera', which Cherubini wrote for the Paris performance in 1792, must have been inserted here.

[2] This was naturally altered according to the town in which the performance took place. Toasting was also very popular in Mozart's opera at a later date; thus in the 1880's in Stuttgart Don Giovanni regularly toasted 'Mozart, the great master'.

to entertain him. When the Commendatore invites Don Giovanni he accepts with a handshake, but rejects his exhortation to do penance and descends among the spirits of Hell to be tortured. When Hell disappears and the hall is seen again, Ottavio, Ximena, Elvira and Maturina return to be told by the servants what has happened, and unite in the usual cheerful finale.

Soon after the Venice performance this *Don Giovanni* must have come to Vienna. It was just at the time when Mozart had to write a new opera for Prague. Very possibly their acquaintance with Bertati's text may have decided da Ponte and Mozart to choose this subject. However it came about, the new work was based on Bertati and da Ponte took not only the principal characters and scenes but even certain words and phrases from his model. Where he changes something, it is easy to see why. As with Figaro, he has again preferred to re-shape an older libretto rather than create his own. And in both instances he undeniably proved his dramatic skill. It is typical of da Ponte as a man that in the case of *Don Giovanni* he not only remained silent about his source but also treated Bertati, who was later to replace him at the Court of Vienna, with scorn and hatred.

Without any doubt, Bertati had raised the plot to a higher and more musical plane. Departing from Molière's and Goldoni's rationalistic treatment, he restored the original impulsive and irrational sensuality characteristic of the old *Burlador* of 1630. Consequently it is far easier to accept the intervention of super-natural powers. The older authors had, from the outset, been faced with the impossibility of reconciling the formal inclusion of mystic and fantastic elements with their 'enlightened' stand-point. Bertati must take the credit for having raised the story from the level of mere farce, into which it had sunk particularly in Germany and Italy, to a higher dramatic and psychological plane. He certainly did not imagine anything other than an opera buffa, and his text is not lacking in moments of downright bluntness — particularly in the 'Hell' scene, a piece in genuine buffo style, and in the finale with its customary popular appeal:

Donne	A a a, io vò cantare
	Io vò mettermi a saltar
D. Ottavio	La Chitarra io vo suonare
Lanterna	Io suonar vò il Contrabasso

Pasquariello	Ancor io per far del chiasso
	Il fagotto vò suonar
Don Ottavio	Tren, tren, trinchete, trinchete trè
Lanterna	Flon, flon, flon, flon, flon, flon.
Pasquariello	Pu, pu, pu, pu, pu, pu, pu.
Tutti	Che bellissima pazzia!
	Che stranissima armonia!
	Così allegro si va a star.

·But these are only minor concessions to public taste: in general Bertati aimed at the refined buffo artistry that had been shown by Lorenzi and Casti, and in fact put a new *Don Giovanni* on the stage. In itself it was not yet a perfect work of art, but it pointed the way. This was certainly not mere chance; heroes whose very greatness lay in their rebellion against law and convention (consider, for instance, Schiller's *Brigands*) were popular figures at the time. People admired their uncontrolled impulses and the way they did not even flinch at challenging the divine powers; they saw superior qualities in what at an earlier date would have been considered plainly criminal. The reason for the popularity of the Don Juan theme at that time is therefore quite clear: this champion of demoniacal sensuality was the living embodiment of protest against all that seemed unnatural in the old rationalistic view of life.

Certainly none of these authors, not even Bertati, thought of elaborating this idea consciously; they aimed at nothing more than an effective opera buffa. But subconsciously Bertati in particular leaned quite distinctly towards the new conception. It is characteristic that he replaced the old subtitle of the 'Dissoluto punito' by the more neutral 'Convitato di pietra': the quod erat demonstrandum, the old magic formula of rationalism, no longer held any attraction for him. He did not want to teach or to convert, or to pass sentence in a trial of Good and Evil, but only to stick to plain reality. He aimed to make the drama effective through its own power, and already, despite all the buffo elements, behind the shape of the final scene there dawns a recognition of tragedy, a tragedy that is based not on crime and punishment, but simply on the impact of the dramatic action. The significance of Bertati for Mozart lay precisely in this kind of inspiration, however much his work may in other ways still stem from tradition.

Practical considerations, especially the limited ability of the singers in Prague, led da Ponte to alter some of the details in Bertati. First of all Lanterna the cook was sacrificed, so that Don Giovanni kept only one servant; then Donna Ximena was cut out, though leaving clear traces of her character in the figure of Donna Elvira and even more in that of Zerlina. This was definitely a step forward, for it meant that the three other women acquired a sharper characterization and dramatically became more effective adversaries of the hero. The same applies to the most far-reaching alteration made by da Ponte: the extension of the part of Donna Anna. In Bertati's version she retires from the opera in the first scene, to await in a convent the vengeance that Ottavio is to exact. Da Ponte, on the other hand, gives her a continuing share in the drama, as Don Giovanni's most resolute adversary, and this significantly deepens both her own and Don Giovanni's characterization.

It has been suggested justifiably by Chrysander that Mozart had a hand in this. In the past he had expressed strong views on the subject of female characters to his librettists; now, in his most mature period, why should he suddenly have refrained from doing so? With the Countess in *Figaro* he had already introduced a character who stood out against her light-hearted environment in darker, deeper shades of feeling and disposition. Did not *Don Giovanni*, with its sharper contrasts, demand a corresponding figure even more strongly? And when we look at the final result, it becomes quite clear that Donna Anna owes her dramatic essence not to the poet but to the musician. Da Ponte contented himself with elaborating what Bertati had already suggested, not changing anything in the fundamental nature of the character, nor adding a single new theme. In consequence, the Donna Anna of the libretto dominates the stage only episodically, whereas Mozart, by his musical characterization, achieved what at all times has been attainable only by the greatest of dramatic musicians; he has by his music transformed a figure left by the poet in vague, half-finished contours, not only into a living and consistent character but also into one of the chief personalities in the whole drama. In view of this it is incomprehensible why in more recent times some people have wanted to deny Mozart any share in the libretto.[1]

---

[1] Schurig II, 170. Schurig points out, quite rightly, that da Ponte improved

Both Bertati and da Ponte left Donna Elvira just as she is in Molière. She has to suffer great humiliation, with Bertati in the quarrel duet with Maturina, with da Ponte in the scene with the disguised Leporello. But in both texts this passionate woman frustrates all the hero's intentions, and with her last cry of warning rises to real greatness of character. Thus Molière's inspired creation has also benefited the opera.

Zerlina, now assimilated with Ximena, is far superior to the rough buffo character of Maturina. Da Ponte endowed her both with innocent grace and with the natural impulsiveness of a simple country girl. One happy inspiration of da Ponte's was her reconciliation with Masetto, which logically rounds off the picture of her character. Masetto too, gains by this. Bertati's Biagio appears only once, just to witness Maturina's faithfulness and then to be thrashed off the stage by Don Giovanni. Masetto's martyrdom is longer and more painful, but for this reason Zerlina's return to him seems more convincing. Each supports the other, and instead of two buffo figures dealt with by the poet in the usual unmerciful way, we have an ordinary loving couple, who despite all kinds of sin and peril find themselves together again in the end. Above all, their connexion with the other characters, in particular with Don Giovanni, becomes much closer and more vital.

With Don Ottavio, Da Ponte has stressed the passive side of his character without ennobling it in any way; and finally, the Commendatore and Leporello, his opposite, are almost entirely modelled on Bertati. The only difference is that with da Ponte Leporello is the only comic character in the opera, while in Bertati almost everyone shares in the comedy to a greater or lesser extent.

We have already discussed Don Giovanni's character in general. Bertati's sketchy delineation probably arose from the one-act

---

the dramatic effect by putting Donna Anna's account of Don Giovanni's assault after the recognition scene. Here, however, he criticizes Mozart, saying that 'the only musical weakness of *Don Giovanni* is the treatment of this important moment in *secco* recitative.' This is a major error, for the so-called *secco* recitative is, in fact, a recitativo *accompagnato* in the grand manner, a form which composers of the period reserved for moments of special significance. Schurig concluded that this passage shows Mozart as a far from clear-thinking dramatist, but in fact it suggests exactly the opposite.

form, while da Ponte was able to work on a larger canvas; but although he paints with a finer brush and in greater detail, he has added nothing significant to Bertati's portrait and the Don does not become a different person.

Therefore Bertati should really be credited with a great deal of the merit for the text formerly ascribed to da Ponte. In one respect da Ponte's procedure was even retrogressive — his stress on rationalistic morality, already shown in the re-introduction of the subtitle *Il dissoluto punito*, calls Goldoni to mind. Da Ponte simply could not conceive of tragedy without this addition. In the course of the piece, it is true, the complications of the plot prevented him from over-emphasizing this feature; and the dramatic poet in him fortunately proved stronger than the moralist. But in the final scene he still could not refrain from drawing a moral. Instead of Bertati's burlesque ending he first brings the destinies of Donna Anna and Elvira to a satisfactory conclusion; but then he tries to do justice to the buffo spirit as well as to the 'tragic moral' by letting everyone join 'allegramente' in the 'antichissima canzon':

> Questo è il fin di che fa mal,
> E de' perfidi la morte alla vita è sempre ugual!

This is the favourite moral ending, belonging less to the opera buffa than to the opéra comique, and all that is missing is the vaudeville tradition by which each character provided further instances to prove the statement.

Nevertheless, da Ponte's contribution should not be underestimated. He is obviously striving to make Bertati's buffo text suit Mozart's unique qualities, for the music of *Figaro* had sharpened his perception considerably. When he set to work on Beaumarchais' comedy, his aim had been to produce an opera buffa, but Mozart's music had taught him that the composer saw his subject with quite different eyes and however vague he may have been about this new artistic ideal, he felt instinctively the form that the poetry should take in order to satisfy the composer. One can see how he elaborates on Bertati's figures with Mozart's dramatic characterization in mind, intensifying and deepening the contrasts between them, and particularly how he develops Bertati's genuinely musical characters to suit Mozart's individuality.

Indeed Mozart had never been and was never again to be pre-

41

sented with characters that accommodated music as well as they did in *Don Giovanni*. This applies to Leporello as well as to the three women, but particularly to the highly individual way in which Don Giovanni himself is characterized. Throughout the opera nothing happens that is not in some way related to him, or to some aspect of his nature; everything centres round him, his actions or his destiny. This is quite different from the many-sidedness of Figaro, yet Don Giovanni has not a single aria of the old type to sing.[1] The famous 'Finch' han dal vino' can only be classed as such up to a point. As a man of action Don Giovanni has no time at all for lyrical effusions; his nature unfolds in interplay with other characters. This was something quite new and extra-ordinary for the time, since it was customary for operatic heroes to present themselves unmistakably to the public in their arias. Now the characterization was indirect, so that the apparently unintentional took the place of the calculated effect. This confronted the composer, too, with a new and difficult task. If the hero was to appear not only as an individual and consistent character, but also as the central figure, if he was to be not only an impulsive adventurer but also an exceptional human being of over-whelming energy, fired by sensual passion — then a musician of more than ordinary creative power was needed to find new means to solve the problem. Mozart's difficulty here was incomparably greater than in *Figaro*, but it was also bound to be an exciting challenge to his all-embracing genius.

From a technical point of view, one cannot deny da Ponte credit for having greatly intensified Bertati's action with effective contrasts, especially in the first act. The second could certainly have done with some new dramatic motive, for the continued pursuit of Don Giovanni hardly appears enough to maintain the tension. However, creative ideas in the grand manner were not da Ponte's forte. To put together his second act, he therefore had recourse to such hackneyed expedients of opera buffa as ex-changing clothes and engineering scuffles, only returning to the grand dramatic style towards the end, from the churchyard scene onwards. All the same, in the second act, the individual situations are visually effective and musically full of potential. And here lies

---

[1] This did not suit the singers of the period. Bertati gives Don Giovanni an aria in the scene with Ximena, which da Ponte extended into a duet.

one of da Ponte's chief virtues: he understood, particularly in the ensembles — Mozart's main achievement — how to construct each scene so that it would be ideal for musical treatment.

When it comes to the poetical expression of passionate emotions, however, others — especially Casti — are certainly superior to him and not much remains in his text of the chivalrous aspect of the Spanish original. At the same time it reveals quite a marked Rococo spirit which could combine unbridled enjoyment of life with humanism and all kinds of mystical ideas. This gives the text its own brand of truthfulness, and the Rococo element also accounts for the elegant and graceful mode of expression which distinguishes da Ponte from the more robust Bertati.

Thus many things come together in this libretto to inspire Mozart's creative powers to an exceptional degree — as in *Figaro*, but in a quite different direction, and with heights and depths of which the earlier work gave hardly a hint. With good reason Goethe said of *Don Giovanni* that Mozart would have been the man to set his *Faust* to music. This judgement was surely not based on the mere similarity of plot, but on the instinctive feeling that here was an artist akin to himself, both in his universality and even more in his whole way of creating an image of the world. Two years later he said: 'How can anyone say that Mozart 'composed' *Don Giovanni*? Composition — as if it were a cake or biscuit, made by mixing eggs, flour and sugar together! It is a spiritual creation — the detail, like the whole, made by one mind in one mould and shot through with the breath of life — in which the author was not experimenting, or piecing together or acting arbitrarily, but had to do as he was bidden by the daemon of his genius.'

Take the action first. Leporello, acting as sentinel, waits impatiently for his master, who has stolen away to a rendez-vous. Don Giovanni enters pursued by Donna Anna, and tries in vain to disengage himself from her. In response to her cries for help the Commendatore enters and compels the intruder to fight a duel; he falls by the hand of Don Giovanni who, like Leporello, is taken aback by the incident.[1] But there is no time to lose; Don Giovanni

---

[1] This is clear from the words 'Ah già cadde il sciagurato' and even more so from the music; it is still faintly discernible in Don Giovanni's words in the second scene.

flees, and immediately Donna Anna returns with her betrothed, Don Ottavio. At the sight of her dead father she is beside herself with grief and faints away. Hardly has she come to her senses than she makes Don Ottavio swear an oath of vengeance.

Don Giovanni pays no attention to Leporello's warnings and is just telling him that he has embarked on a new adventure, when a lady joins them. This is Donna Elvira, who has been seduced and then abandoned by Don Giovanni in Burgos and has followed him to remind him of his pledge: he steps towards her and is very disconcerted to recognize her.[1] She overwhelms him with reproaches; he refers her to Leporello for explanations, and uses the opportunity to withdraw. Leporello, by way of consolation, shows her the long catalogue that he keeps of his master's conquests. Indignant at this latest insult she resolves to renounce her love for this faithless man and take vengeance.

Masetto and Zerlina are to celebrate their wedding with their peasant friends near Don Giovanni's country house, where he has come to keep another appointment. The young Zerlina attracts him; he makes the acquaintance of the bride and bridegroom, invites the whole party to his house, and sends Masetto, whose jealousy is aroused, somewhat forcibly away. He is just about to win Zerlina over by flattering her and declaring his love for her, when Elvira steps between them, warns Zerlina and, while Don Giovanni whispers to her that Elvira is a poor demented woman, jealous because of her own love for him, leads her away.[2] Don Giovanni, left behind, is joined by Donna Anna and Don Ottavio, who greet him as a friend of the family and ask his help in finding the murderer of the Commendatore and bringing him to judgment. While Don Giovanni speaks of his concern to Donna Anna, Elvira again intervenes and brands him as a hypocrite. He can see no other way out than to explain quietly that she is out of her senses, and that he ought to leave with her to calm her down. Donna

---

[1] Da Ponte makes no mention of marriage or betrothal to Don Giovanni; he refers to her only as 'abbandonata da Don Giovanni' while in Bertati's text she appears as 'sposa promessa di D.G.'

[2] The supposed madness of Elvira comes from Goldoni and Bertati and is a familiar feature of the opera buffa. But da Ponte used it skilfully to bring together characters only partly known to each other and to arrive at the recognition of Don Giovanni.

Anna, who has become suspicious, watches Don Giovanni closely, recognizes him as her father's murderer, tells Don Ottavio the whole story and calls on him for revenge. Though he cannot immediately believe so grave a suspicion, he does resolve to make searching enquiries about Don Giovanni. The latter, having freed himself from Elvira, now commands a feast to be prepared in honour of the betrothed couple.

Masetto, whom Zerlina has to some extent reassured by taking pains to flatter him, hides as he sees Don Giovanni approaching. Zerlina affects to be prudish, and when Masetto unexpectedly reappears Don Giovanni quickly collects himself; he persuades them both to join the festivities at his house. Donna Anna and Don Ottavio arrive with Elvira, who has told them everything; at her suggestion they are all masked, so as to observe Don Giovanni without being recognized. Leporello notices them and, as expected, invites them to take part in the feast, to which they consent. It was part of the custom in those days, particularly in Venice, to go about masked and to invite such strangers to any festivities in progress; the disguise lifted all formal constraints.

They happen to enter the hall just as there is a pause in the dancing. Refreshments are being handed round, and Don Giovanni is talking to Zerlina while the jealous Masetto tries to warn her, when the arrival of the masked guests attracts general attention; they are greeted gaily, and the dancing begins again. As Mozart explicitly prescribes, Donna Anna and Don Ottavio join in a minuet, the dance of the aristocracy.[1] Donna Anna can barely suppress her revulsion, but Don Ottavio urges her as they dance to control herself. Elvira never lets Don Giovanni out of her sight. He, meanwhile, asks Zerlina for a contre-danse, and Leporello, to divert Masetto's attention from Zerlina, forces him to join in a 'German' dance, a quick lively measure popular with the village people. At an opportune moment Don Giovanni abducts Zerlina and Leporello follows him quickly in order to warn him; at that

---

[1] At masked balls in Hamburg members of the noble families used to demand that in addition to English dances an occasional minuet should be performed 'because they did not want to mix with the crowd'. Mozart's words, 'Don Ottavio balla minuetto con Donna Anna' do not appear in the Prague manuscript. For this and some private reason Wolzogen was opposed to the noble guests dancing: Gugler, too, omitted Mozart's words, quite without justification.

moment her cry for help is heard and everyone rushes to her aid. Don Giovanni meets them, dragging Leporello along. He accuses him of being the culprit and threatens to kill him. But now the masks are dropped and he finds himself confronted on all sides by people he well knows are resolved to take vengeance. Master and servant falter for an instant; then the former defiantly breaks through his enemies and escapes. Distant thunder is heard.

In the second act Don Giovanni pacifies the discontented Leporello with money and friendly words. He confesses that he is pursuing Elvira's pretty maid, and in order to gain access to her, wishes to change clothes with him. No sooner has this been done than Elvira appears at the window. To get her decently out of the way, Don Giovanni amuses himself by renewing his protestations of love with simulated fervour, which she is weak enough to trust. The disguised Leporello now has to hear and to answer her cries of passion, until Don Giovanni rushes noisily in and drives them off. He now tries to lure the chambermaid with a tender song. At this moment Masetto and several friends come in armed, to call Don Giovanni to account; the supposed Leporello promises to put him on the right track and skilfully contrives to disperse the company; he then talks Masetto into giving up his weapons, beats him thoroughly and escapes. Hearing Masetto's cries, Zerlina hurries in and consoles him with her caresses.

Meanwhile Leporello and Elvira have taken refuge in the ante-room of Donna Anna's house;[1] Leporello tries to steal away, but Elvira implores him not to leave her alone in the dark. He is just about to escape when Donna Anna arrives with Don Ottavio, trying to soothe her grief; now Elvira and Leporello both try to get away without the other noticing, but Zerlina and Masetto block their path. Straightaway the supposed Don Giovanni is to be put on trial; to everyone's suprise, Elvira pleads for mercy, but in vain; Leporello reveals himself, tries to justify his actions and luckily manages to escape. Don Ottavio, who no longer doubts that Don Giovanni is the Commendatore's murderer, declares that

---

[1] Da Ponte says explicitly 'Atrio terréno oscuro in casa di Donna Anna'. Edward J. Dent (*Mozart's Operas*) presumes that da Ponte had originally planned an opera in three acts, had thought of the sextet as the second finale, and that Mozart too had a finale in mind when he wrote it. However, this plan may have been laid aside for lack of time.

he will invoke the powers of the law to bring him to justice; he entreats his friends to console his beloved until he has obtained reparation for her.[1]

Near the memorial to the Commendatore Don Giovanni, who has been waiting for Leporello, is laughing over his most recent adventures when an invisible voice twice utters sinister words of warning. He now notices the Commendatore's statue and asks Leporello to read the inscription: 'Here I wait to take vengeance on my wicked murderer'. With utter scorn for Leporello's terror he makes him invite the statue to supper. The statue nods and as Don Giovanni sees this, he himself challenges it to answer; when it actually says 'Yes' he hurries away in dismay.

Don Ottavio again tries to console Donna Anna by announcing Don Giovanni's imminent punishment. He begs her to marry him, but she declares that despite the strength of her feelings for him, her grief for her father forces her to delay the fulfilment of her desires. This scene looks very much as if it had been inserted in Prague after the opera was completed, in order to give Donna Anna a final aria. And the same can be said of Don Ottavio's aria at the end of the Finale, which is not consistent with his behaviour in the preceding scene.

Don Giovanni sits down at his richly appointed table and enjoys a few hearty jokes with Leporello. This scene in which it was traditional for master and servant to indulge in uninhibited foolery, has been used by Mozart as an occasion for some musical jokes. Don Giovanni has musicians at his dinner, who perform popular pieces from the latest operas. At the first few bars Leporello exclaims, 'Bravi! Cosa rara!'. It is the final section of the first Finale in Martin's *Cosa rara*: 'O quanto un si bel guibilo', which everyone was whistling at the time; and the situation is most delicately parodied. There the unlucky suitors see their beloveds snatched away by their rivals before their very eyes; here Leporello hungrily watches Don Giovanni feasting, so that the music seems

---

[1] In the first performance in Vienna this scene was altered, or rather extended. Leporello is caught, dragged back by his hair by Zerlina and tied to a chair; left alone, he tears himself free and escapes. Zerlina, Masetto and Elvira return; Masetto reports Don Giovanni's latest misdeed and runs away with Zerlina to tell Don Ottavio. Elvira remains and, torn between pity and the desire for revenge, breaks into a lament.

to be made for the scene. Leporello cheerfully acclaims the second piece with 'Evvivano i litiganti!' It is Mingone's popular aria in Sarti's opera *Fra due litiganti il terzo gode*, on which Mozart had written a set of variations. Its text, which was then well known, fits Leporello's behaviour in a very comical way:

'Come un agnello
Che va al macello
Andrai belando
Per la città!'

As was usual at the time, these musical inserts, which correspond to Bertati's *brindisi* to the beautiful Venetian ladies, contain not only an element of parody but also a compliment to the appropriate composer. The equally humorous wind scoring is very characteristic of contemporary *Tafelmusik*. Finally, to please his beloved Prague audience, Mozart quotes his own 'Non più andrai' from *Figaro*, and Leporello comments: 'Questa poi la conosco pur troppo!' It is a pleasant gesture of gratitude for the enthusiastic reception of his opera in Prague.

The party is interrupted by Elvira. She has renounced the Don's love and is about to enter a convent, but first wants to try once again to make him repent. However, since his only reply to her pleading is mockery, she regretfully leaves him. Outside she utters a fearful cry; Leporello rushes after her and comes back again trembling with terror: the statue of the Commendatore is at the door. It knocks for Don Giovanni himself to go and open, and return with his stone guest. The Commendatore refuses all hospitality and asks Don Giovanni whether he is prepared to accept an invitation from him; when the reply is in the affirmative he takes his hand and tells him to do penance. As Don Giovanni stubbornly refuses several times, the statue disappears; night falls, flames shoot up from the trembling earth and invisible spirits raise their terrifying voices. They surround Don Giovanni and he is swallowed up in the abyss. Just as he is snatched from mortal vengeance, Don Ottavio, Donna Anna, Elvira, Zerlina and Masetto arrive to punish the evil-doer; Leporello, who has anxiously witnessed the horrible scene, tells them of his master's gruesome end. Their troubles over and rightful relationships restored, they all unite in a moral conclusion.

The idea of Don Giovanni's having no success with any of the women he pursues is taken from Bertati; da Ponte has only made it clearer. But it is hardly, as Jahn would like us to believe, the cause of the 'gaiety which permeates the whole opera'. It should rather be regarded as a very effective element in the characterization of the hero. A character such as his has to be strengthened by continual opposition; his energy is kept in a state of constant tension, driving him to his fate. Besides, the main point of Don Giovanni's nature is not his ability to seduce this or that woman who happens to cross his path, even if there were 'a thousand and three', but in the elemental, sensual urge to live and love which he has the uncontrolled energy to satisfy. The more he reveals himself the more dangerous, but also the greater, he becomes.

Again, it is dramatically telling, and strongly symbolic, that Don Giovanni confronts the Commendatore both at the beginning and at the end of the opera. Already that first scene leads us into the realm of tragedy. We are shaken by Don Giovanni's terrifying nature, which makes him appear as a lord over life and death at the very beginning of the opera. And yet even this does not tax him to the limits of his power. The life of an old man is easy prey for him; he simply takes it as the right of a stronger man. But his attitude towards the statue is quite different; here he is confronted by a power remote from his own world of the senses, which represents a stronger reality than his own. We should not, however, try to see this as a manifestation of a moral law in Schiller's sense. In the second Finale the struggle is not between good and evil, but between two supreme realities of which the weaker succumbs. Mozart, being entirely unphilosophical, knows nothing radically evil at all; he therefore does not assess the hero and his deeds according to an ethical ideal, but feels that a force of such reality as Don Giovanni's can only be overcome by a still more powerful reality, that the one daemon can only be conquered by another daemon. So the drama is not about crime and punishment; it is again a question of 'to be or not to be'. The shattering tragedy of the end lies in the grandeur and terror of the incident as such, not in the triumph of moral law over the world of appearances. Again, the genuine Renaissance spirit shows itself in Don Giovanni, and this follows logically from Mozart's picture of the world where reality is measured only in relation to itself, not according to external philosophically constructed laws.

Because of this, in *Don Giovanni* more than in any of his other operas he has gone far beyond the librettist and his conceptions, despite the fact that the poet had tried so hard to adjust himself to Mozart's individuality. To such an extent is the opera, as a whole and in its detail, essentially Mozart's creation that the text in this case is merely like a frame round which a sculptor creates his model, and the score is an unprecedented triumph for his dramatic and musical imagination.[1]

For the overture Mozart chose the French form, combining a slow movement with a fast one — as in all his subsequent operas — but it is not as if he had changed his attitude to the overture as such. As before, it remains an instrumental piece to introduce the listener to the emotional atmosphere of the drama to follow, but not into the course of the action itself; and for this reason it will not bear particular poetic interpretations such as the nineteenth century, with its intellectualizing, continually tried to impose on it. It is indeed a piece that is quite unequivocal as regards music or sentiment.

It differs from the *Figaro* overture only in so far as that opera had a uniform emotional basis, while here it is governed by two fundamental opposites. So the binary form suggested itself quite naturally to Mozart, although he is content merely to state the contrasts and to leave the argument to the opera itself. Certainly there is an inner connexion between the Andante and the Allegro; but we must not regard the former, according to the usual convention, as a 'slow introduction' to the latter. There is absolutely nothing to 'introduce', but with a frightening clarity typical of the whole opera, one of the two fundamental forces of the drama bursts on us with elemental power, doubly terrifying in its laconic

---

[1] The original score was acquired by Mme Viardot and was bequeathed to the Paris Conservatoire after her death. Prochazka refers to a second, so-called original score which, however, is probably a copy made in Prague under Mozart's supervision. The first edition of the score based on the autograph was arranged through B. Gugler by Leuckart in Breslau in 1870. The next was brought out by Julius Rietz with Breitkopf & Härtel, 1872. This edition also forms the basis of the Gesamtausgabe.

brevity, and already proving itself not merely equal to the other, but superior. But this other also has a harsh, breathtakingly demoniacal quality, besides something primaeval and volcanic that is remote from the world of the *Figaro* overture, and this impression is intensified by the fact that the *Andante* always hangs over it like a cloud. The nature of the two contrasting ideas the composer wishes the listener to experience is expressed musically with such lucidity that only intellectual hairsplitting could obscure it. We have here not two portraits, faithful in every detail, of the Stone Guest and Don Giovanni, but on the one hand the representation of a power terrifying in its sublimity, with its blood-chilling aura of another world, and on the other a demoniacal passion spurred on to ever greater heights by every resistance it meets. This is all the unprejudiced listener will feel, and it is all that Mozart intended. Yet the relentless energy with which this contrast has been worked out is intensely exciting for the listener; without knowing anything about the struggle itself or its outcome he senses that there can be no reconciliation between these two superhuman forces. This tension is so important to Mozart that, rather than shatter the aesthetic image with a final cadence, he allows the picture to fade out gradually as if a delicate veil were descending, and the overture leads straight into the first scene.

This is therefore not a programme overture, either in the old Venetian or in the later romantic sense, and if Mozart in the Andante used the music of the ghost scene, it was not in order to conjure up the *convitato di pietra* in person, but because it seemed natural to him to employ the same music to symbolize the supernatural power represented in the opera by the Stone Guest. His tragic key, D minor,[1] is used in both cases, except that in the overture, where particular events play no part, it dominates the whole even more inexorably than in the opera; however far and wide the series of modulations moves, the music always returns to it as if guided by some magic force.

As in the opera, the supernatural power is heralded by a four-bar introduction. There are only two chords for full orchestra, tonic and dominant, yet what a shattering impact is made by the momentous silence that follows each chord and by the incomparable effect of the syncopation, further intensified by the

---

[1] Mozart's very first 'tragic' overture, to *Betulia liberata*, is also in D minor.

strangely resounding minims on the basses! We feel as if a contorted Medusa were staring at us. Only then does the actual development begin, in which the music of the later scene is compressed to its utmost. No theme is at all broadly extended;[1] as if in a mist, disembodied images of terror and grief pass before us; they lack the plastic and tangible quality which the stage appearance is to provide later. Moreover, there is something elemental in the general character of the melodic lines. They consist largely of motifs which seem like interjections or natural sounds. Apart from the harmony, the character of the movement is for the most part determined by rhythm, dynamics and orchestral colouring.[2]

And yet all the ideas which externally contrast so sharply with one another have a distinct inner connexion, as one stroke always provokes a counter-stroke. After those two forte introductory chords the other world begins to make itself heard, piano (this is the first of the dynamic contrasts in which the overture is so rich). The harmony moves with decisive firmness in heavy dotted rhythms over a bass line descending chromatically through a fourth; while above, the gigantic motif in octaves is heard in ever-changing combinations of wind instruments, from flutes to horns and trumpets. But then follows the counter-stroke; the unyielding syncopated melody in the first violins (bar 11), is soon joined by a dark, murmuring semiquaver figure in the seconds, as if the wind were stirring up faded leaves.[3] And so it goes on: in a short, harsh sforzato motif,[4] consisting of only two notes, the voice from the

---

[1] In this the Introduction is very different even from similar pieces in Mozart's instrumental works.

[2] This shows quite clearly the influence of Gluck.

[3] The whole atmosphere is reminiscent of those scenes at the gates of Hell which occur so frequently in Italian opera and in Gluck (e.g. *Alceste*). Their vivid portrayal of that mysterious, awe-inspiring world, with their *orribili* or *flebili accenti* in the woodwind, is clearly paralleled here, except that Mozart transforms the mere depicting of a situation into something genuinely psychological and emotional.

[4]   The first time in this simple form:

the second time extended:

A version half-way between the two   concludes this section.

other world seems to speak more and more dauntingly, followed each time by the anxious response of a troubled soul which at the end, completely broken, submits to fate (bars 21-22). Then in the second section, stroke and counter-stroke come together.

The dotted rhythm of the beginning now returns in the bass, which this time moves up instead of down a fourth and pulls the harmony with it in a sequence of chromatically rising chords of the sixth. To this — over a tremolo in the second violins and violas — the first violins and flutes add the well-known scale passages, which make the listener feel an almost physical dread of the Eternal. The scales rise in a crescendo, then flow downwards again piano — the effect should not be weakened by inserting a diminuendo! Similarly there should be no transitional crescendo in bars 23-27. The tension here lies solely in the harmonic progression, not in the dynamics. Then the effect of the forte in bar 27, the climax of the passage when the scales also stop, is all the more terrifying. But hardly has the spine-chilling supernatural power entered than it disappears again in a sudden piano, whose effect derives mainly from a dynamic twist of the motif in the wind instruments:

The dynamics of the whole movement are pure Mozart. He gives the listener only three bars[1] to let the awesome experience fade away; then virtually unprepared, he is faced with the most abrupt change imaginable in the Allegro. With the instinct of genius Mozart follows D minor with D major: the purely musical change of mode on the same tonic serves perfectly to connect the two sections as well as to contrast them vividly. The Allegro itself is a fully developed sonata movement this time, unlike the *Figaro* overture; it is therefore not a succession of different elements that would preclude any lingering on individual ideas, but a probing into and intensification of forces latent in the principal themes, moving, not one beside or after the other, but within or against one another.

Much has been written about the character of the Allegro

---

[1] Even the third bar (the first of the Allegro) with its empty fifth leaves the actual mode still in the balance, holding the attention for what is to follow only with softly hammering D's in the violas and cellos.

theme and the Romantics in particular wanted to identify every motif with a different facet of Don Giovanni's character; his demonic sensuality in the chromatic step, his impetuous energy in the syncopation, his levity in the quaver figure and his cavalier temperament in the concluding wind passage.[1] But, as has already been said, this is reading much too much into it. After all, we are not dealing with a musical portrait of Don Giovanni, to which every bar adds a new stroke of the brush — quite apart from the fact that such mosaic-like piecing together goes against all the precepts of musical creation. No, this theme, one of Mozart's most ingenious ideas, has been created at one stroke and needs to be taken in at one stroke. Its first half:

shows, without any need for intellectual interpretation, what is presented clearly in the emotional substance of the music: the pressure and release of a prodigious vital energy. This is the fundamental element that holds the whole diverse creation together. But over this many-sidedness rules a strong formative will, as is proved by the rhythm and metre, which the listener at once recognizes as peculiar and original. Every motif[2] starts with an upbeat,[3] always consisting of two notes which are then followed by the main accent. This is the basic character of anapaestic rhythm, which since the days of antiquity has been regarded as a symbol of the life force. Until the fourth bar it remains latent, so to speak, having to prevail against the pressure of the heavy upbeats and also to overcome, in motifs b^2 and c, the break-up of its accentuated beat into quavers, before it can emerge in its true form with the daemonic fanfare on the wind instruments. So what happens in this theme, through the progressive shortening of the upbeats, is a uniform and constantly intensified inner development: a force under strong pressure gradually breaking though to its full deployment.

This psychological process is reinforced in the most impressive way by the melody and the harmony. The melodic element is the

---

[1] The originator of all these interpretations is E.T.A. Hoffmann.
[2] See the letters and brackets under the musical example above.
[3] The motif 'a' is also a *Generalauftakt*, according to H. Riemann.

first hidden resistance this force has to overcome. Consider, for instance, the famous D♯ in the second bar, with its incisive dissonance driving the harmony at the very beginning into the relative minor of the subdominant and considerably increasing the tension of motif 'a'. In the 'b' group the rhythmic intensification also seems at first to influence the melody, but the initial surge of energy is always followed by a downward curve in the melodic line, and the more the rhythmic intensity grows, the more stubbornly something pulls the melody back to the tonic; the small suspensions are the last resistance if offers. Only in group 'd' is this barrier lifted, and the fifth (A) is easily reached, underlining the explosive character of the passage. In the first five bars the harmony moves over a tonic pedal. However, this is in no sense a typical Neapolitan drum bass, as is evident from its scoring for violas and cellos alone (without double basses). The hammering on the high D in the bass, after the weighty chromatic progression in the Andante, has a strangely glittering and provocative effect, like a sudden change from icy cold to burning heat. The pedal note itself proves to be the main source of energy in the first half of the theme. In group 'b' the harmony is left in a state of uncertainty since the composer regards the reinforcement of the melodic line by the lower sixth and third as more important; only in the second half of the theme does the latent dominant harmony become apparent. In the third bar from the end the tension is also released in energetic cadential steps, and now in the violent outburst of the two final bars — in which dynamics and orchestration combine with rhythm and melody — the harmony also plays a part through the lapidary style in which it strains towards the dominant. It really feels as if the long-restrained fires of passion suddenly surge upwards to the sky.

Therefore this theme, if only its metrical structure is correctly understood, speaks for itself and has no need of poetical interpretation. Its second half resembles the first except that the pedal note is strengthened by the horns and the harmony is completely filled in by the woodwind, in order to increase the emotional effect.[1] The impetus of the final bars, though, is no longer carried

[1] In earlier published editions there is a flat before the B in the fourth bar, which the original shows only in the third. There has been much argument about this; Gugler puts a flat both times, but Pietz a natural both times, as does the *Gesamtausgabe*. Neither is authentic. In the third bar we have an

by the wind fanfare, but by a more elaborate and emotionally much
more intense passage for the whole orchestra. It is based on the
same anapaestic rhythm with powerful unisons, storming up to D
and leading to an abrupt, almost brutal half-close. This is the way
the school of J.C. Bach used to introduce its subsidiary themes,
and indeed a new idea does appear, in A major. But it provides no
fundamental contrast; instead there are defiant strokes on the full
orchestra, from which scales detach themselves three times. Here
again there is no lack of counteraction, as is shown by the little
melody for the wind, once more over a pedal note in the strings;
but this serves only to calm the storm for a moment, since it
rages all the more savagely later on.[1] And that happens with the
usual abruptness — for the overture does not contain a transitional
crescendo anywhere — in a diminished chord which leads to A
minor instead of A major. This minor key, which is also to play
an important part in the subsidiary theme, gives the underlying
sensual drive a particular violence that we also feel in Don
Giovanni's aria (No. 12). Here again the end of the phrase is a
defiant half-close, this time on the dominant of A minor. Only
now does the actual subsidiary theme enter, strikingly articulated
and, in true Mozartian manner, dominated by harsh contrasts of
melody and orchestration:[2] This theme, too, has become the

victim of poetical interpretation, the first half being explained as
the warning of the Stone Guest, and the second as Don Giovanni's
flippant reply. This shows once more the desire to find an immediate connexion between the overture and the characters or events
in the opera at any price, perfectly justifiable with the works of

accompanying part which can well be dramatically altered since the B♭ is
prepared by the C natural in the second bar; in the fourth bar, however, the
principal theme must return to its original shape and we therefore have no
right to make a change for the sake of being academically consistent.

[1] Merian sees this passage as representing Don Giovanni's escapade with
Zerlina!
[2] The alleged derivation of this theme and its imitative elaboration from the
Kyrie of Stölzel's *Missa canonica*, which the North Germans Marpurg and
Kirnberger claimed to discover, has long been recognized as sheer reminis-
cence-hunting.

Weber and his time, but not with Mozart. Why should he suddenly introduce a dialogue between two people from the opera itself? If he had wanted such a thing, this born master of contrasts would surely have underlined the renewed intervention of the supernatural in quite a different musical way from that of the preceding themes, instead of simply continuing on the dominant, without any harmonic change. No: this subsidiary theme does not introduce a change of scene, and provides no contrast at all to what went before, being related to it as fulfilment is to preparation. It is the old daemonic impulse that now manifests itself with redoubled force. Characteristically, Mozart presents this theme in the form of two opposites, one of which immediately calls for the other. The wild obstinacy of the unison sforzato motif gives the answer to what has gone before, as if a heavy load had been shaken off. But the theme, with its dominant seventh harmony, also points the way ahead, and the answer comes in the quaver figure. Here the anapaestic rhythm from group 'c' of the main theme again appears — a further proof of the inner connexion between the two thematic groups. Instead of 'frivolous dallying' there is again the expression of intense energy that is the anwer we expect to the defiant challenge. Even the double basses, who were absent in the principal theme, are not left out.

So the subsidiary theme stresses, somehow, the two extreme aspects of the life energy: stubborn belligerency and self satisfied delight in its own manifestation. At first the aggressive mood has the upper hand in a three-part canon. But in a surprising turn to C major which suddenly sheds a completely different light on everything the motif loses its sforzato and the imitations become freer. The driving force has begun to flag, and now unfolds one of those truly Mozartian, apparently relaxed and yet frightening moments of tension:[1] the psychologically apt recoil, after the preceding concentration of force. Yet this is only the calm before the storm; the sudden forte of the concluding group in A major overrides the subsidiary theme and returns to the violence of the principal group, of which it is also motivically reminiscent. Finally it builds up to the exposition's cadential section, and the irresistible display of force has the last word.

---

[1] N.B.the sombre murmuring of the violins and above all the augmented fourth in the flutes.

The development section begins with the subsidiary theme, again without the change of key that is so frequent in Mozart's works precisely at this point; but its two contrasting phrases are connected in so far as the basic harmony remains the same; the 'answer' appears only with the repeat of the whole theme in the fifth bar. Then the canonic imitations begin again, but now over a wide harmonic arch, which, by making each key the dominant of the next leads through the whole territory of the neighbouring 'sharp' tonalities to G major. Meanwhile the second motif of the theme continually flares up in the strings, causing stringent dissonances with its suspension.[1] It is the most inspired moment in the whole Allegro and shows clearly that the two opposites are fundamentally manifestations of the same force. And the whole episode is marked piano; full of drama as it is, it leaves no feeling of a struggle. But when we reach the subdominant, G major, everything is changed; the main theme, with its latent conflicts and shrill fanfares, appears once more. It is not completed, however; the second half veers round to G minor and from there deep into the realm of the subdominant, which Mozart at that period loved to explore in his developments. At the same time it gradually loses all its energy and collapses somewhat helplessly onto the dominant of Bb major — again one of those strikingly effective passages in which the tension is relaxed.

Here, too, as in the rest of the overture, there is no gradual recovery of strength, but only the impulsive breaking loose of a terrifying power: one feels distinctly that influences are at work that transcend human measure. The subsidiary theme achieves what was denied the principal theme. It enters six times with its full weight,[2] changing pitch each time, quite stark without any imitations and simply setting its two contrary elements against one another, the first three notes accompanied by shrill chords on all the wind instruments and a timpani roll. Nor are the six entries harmonically of equal significance. The first stands entirely by itself, the next four two by two in the relationship of dominant

[1] Only the end of the motif is new: the two ascending crotchets produce a certain similarity with the corresponding passage in the first movement of the G minor Symphony.
[1] The sf has been replaced here by a real f.

and tonic.[1] The last one seems to continue the procedure but diverges in its final bar; this is the climax of the development section where the level of thought is at its most intense. Again there is no gradual transition, but after a singular whispering passage (without the double basses) the return to the recapitulation comes with violent sforzati and a forte outburst in the whole orchestra, with the insertion — true Mozart again — of a scale passage in the violins, rippling softy downwards. The recapitulation itself, in contrast to most other sonata movements of the period, follows almost exactly the same course as the exposition until the surprising twist away to the subdominant near the end; the savage battle-cry of the subsidiary theme is heard again in the full orchestra,[2] to disappear at once, like its counterpart in the Andante, as if behind a veil.

This powerful prologue, which represents the two opposing forces of fate with unrelenting harshness,[4] is immediately followed, without any break in the aesthetic mood, by the no less powerful Introduction (No. 1). This extends dramatically as far as the beginning of the fourth scene. It is extraordinary to see what the librettist, and especially the composer, have made of the old closely-knit buffo introduction, with its extravagant joviality. Instead of a prelude we are at once faced with a climax of the first order. Already the 'dramma giocoso' of the title page is cruelly given the lie, despite the fact that the one comic character of the piece appears straight away in the first of the four movements of which the Introduction consists. Of course Leporello has long since ceased to be the servo ridiculo of the old story, who made jokes throughout the action rather than taking part in it. He is now a thoroughly individual character in an entirely Mozartian way, his inner nature being revealed in interplay with the other characters. It was already clear in Mozart's earlier operas that he

---

[2] The sequence of harmonies in this part is as follows: B flat - g^V - g^I (= d^{IV}) - d^V - d^I (= a^{IV}) - a^V - A^I. Observe the minor keys! (Capital letters signify major, small letters minor keys.)

[2] It is significant that this motif appears every time in a different orchestration.

[3] Nägeli severely criticizes this 'exaggerated and excessive contrast', which of course extends to the thematic detail, and he considers bars 36 and 197 as superfluous, disturbing the rhythmic balance. A concert ending in Mozart's hand, evidently scribbled out in great hurry, is attached to the autograph.

always saw his characters in relation to one another; he models each one, and each entire group, with regard to the light or shade thrown by the others, so that every character is not only an individual but also a measure of comparison for all the others.

Leporello is one of the most inspired examples of this method, for he owes this whole dramatic existence to his lord and master. To start with, he takes over all Don Giovanni's comic attributes, which are still evident even in Bertati's version. For Mozart such a thing was impossible. Count Almaviva might still contain both tragic and comic elements; but with Don Giovanni the grandeur of the dramatic argument would not allow it. He had to pass to Leporello all those features of his image that might reduce it to the finite and all too human. This determines the character of Leporello and his whole position in the opera. His nature is definitely similar to his master's; he differs from him only in representing a different degree of reality. Don Giovanni's world is that of primaeval and therefore timeless existence, while Leporello is satisfied with the superficial side of living, the common reality of every day. He remains always a dependent, the play-thing of chance and of his position. All that is real in his master is only apparent in him. The gigantic destiny that is fulfilled in Don Giovanni passes him by, and his whole existence remains quite insignificant, being entirely governed by casual adventures. Basically he is a good-natured everyday character, with some country shrewdness. Like all people of his kind he is inclined to moralize but is also capable of sentimental impulses; therefore he tries again and again to cut loose from his dangerous and uncertain position and to find the peace that he secretly craves. But it was a drop of Don Giovanni's blood in his own veins that had led him to his side, and it stirs in him constantly, making him thoroughly wily, someone who from the very beginning flirts with the idea of playing the master himself one day. This side of his character frustrates all his philistine intentions and compels him in the end to go on following his master, as a shadow follows light. Once in a while he preaches to Don Giovanni on the subject of morals, which he immediately violates by his actions. Anxious or indignant as he may be about the tricks that are forced on him, in his heart of hearts he quite enjoys them. So he is hardly less unscrupulous and cunning than his master. Even his craven spirit should not be overstressed, as it so often is. Nothing was further from Mozart's mind than to draw him as the 'typical coward'. His Leporello behaves in character even when in danger; he has not enough pluck to look for trouble or to risk his life, but he is resourceful enough to extricate himself with skill — Don Giovanni would hardly have chosen a coward for his servant. Only when faced with the Stone Guest does Leporello begin to quake with fear. The supernatural impresses him as it would a character such as his; it also affects Don Giovanni in an equally appropriate way. Don Giovanni, the man of exceptional attributes, inspires fear and terror as he grows greater and more dangerous; Leporello, always the bearer of stale news, emerges from the same situations as a poor knave, a bragging, equivocal, contemptible fellow. His relationship with Don Giovanni whirls him past all the other characters of the drama in turn and brings him up against passions and events that his mind is quite unable to fathom — in the end he remains much the same rogue as at the beginning. Leporello's comicality rests on this inner relationship with Don Giovanni, and thus far transcends the old clownish jokes. He is the character in contrast with the hero, as seen by the eye of a genius. What is to be a fatal event for his master, remains for him something purely accidental, within the bounds of common actuality. Anything rising to a tragic level in Don Giovanni ends for him in comedy; and Mozart has again demonstrated the truth of the old saying that only the true tragedian can be a genuine comic.

In the famous 'Notte e giorno faticar', whose melody immortalizes what is a traditional Italian type of tune, Leporello complains about a servant's lot, while he trudges angrily up and down, showing a good deal of temperament in the surly way he rounds off his phrases. But this outburst of anger is only the introduction to the section beginning 'voglio far il gentiluomo', (once more in ternary form) in which the Don Giovanni side of his character stirs for the first time. His cavalier-like swagger is delightfully expressed by the accompanying triplets and the sound of horns, and there are quite unmistakable echoes from the exciting world of Don Giovanni in the little wind passage after 'gentiluomo' and in the short interlude before 'O che caro galant uomo'. At first 'e non voglio più servir' maintains this mood, but at once in the answering passage the spark of ambition fades, giving way to what

61

lies nearest, the workaday misery that overwhelms him again and finds bitter manifestation in a style that is reminiscent of Piccinni.[1] It is typical that from now on this afterthought rounds off every section, like a refrain, in ill-humoured 'ceterum censeo', even when the noise from inside the house makes him hide. With a short and explosive crescendo run into B flat major the scene changes. The music here was obviously suggested by Gazzaniga, but nothing more. Only the tumultuous opening motif and the dotted rhythm of the first vocal phrases are the same; otherwise Mozart has extended and deepened the whole piece in its form and scope, and particularly in its dramatic expression. The form is abbreviated binary, with an introduction that is thematically connected with what follows. The fact that it is not Don Giovanni (as in Bertati) but Donna Anna who speaks first is not without significance, because it reveals at once a very important side of his character, namely the remarkable way in which he adjusts himself musically to the manner of the woman with whom he has to deal. This makes his daemonism all the more dangerous; he attracts his victims even musically and so touches them in their innermost being. He answers Donna Anna with equally passionate indignation and clings closely to her, particularly in the wildly excited 'Come furia disperata'. Here the imitative treatment adds incomparably to the picture of the struggle, in which the couple finally seem to run out of breath. How very different from Gazzaniga, where Don Giovanni sets the pace in order, incidentally, to come together musically with Leporello later on! Mozart quite logically separates Leporello from the struggling pair and puts him, so to speak, on a completely different level inside the same picture. His vocal line is also far more realistic. When he has recovered from his first fright, he has, in contrast to the other two, only broken triads to sing, first in crotchets, then in quick chattering quavers; he always enters piano, when a climax in the duel between the other two is followed by a breathing-space. The difference between the world of the protagonist and that of this workaday rogue could not have been presented more vividly. The champion of deeds and the champion of words! Since Leporello chatters twice as much to air his small mind, Mozart gives him the old buffo-type parlando.

---

[1] The way the accompaniment of triplets and horns ceases is also significant.

Now follows another of the abrupt and violent transitions in which this opera is so rich. Donna Anna breaks loose from Don Giovanni and hurries away. The Commendatore's entrance now begins the third section of the introduction, in which the choice of keys is significant. G minor, which appears first, is for Mozart not at all the key of tragic pathos, but of passionate grief. It represents at this moment the character of the old man. Only when he has forced a duel on his adversary does the tragic D minor spread its shadow over the two combatants. The Commendatore enters, however, in a dignified and determined fashion.[1] Curtly and decisively Don Giovanni at first refuses the unequal fight which goes against his code of chivalry. But with the sinister piano unisons in the orchestra, which in Mozart always signify a special tension and in this case make the final move into D minor, fatality moves nearer; with cruel irony Leporello, with his particular dislike for decisions involving life and death, intervenes. Once again Don Giovanni hesitates with his 'Misero!', at first sotto voce, then più voce, but one must not regard this as a gentler impulse, only as an expression of regret that his adversary is not equal to him. The high point of tension lies in the silent bar, which really seems to stop the heart beating. Then Don Giovanni breaks out again with his 'Misero!', forte this time. These eight bars, including the silent one, are the climax of the whole Introduction: here the fateful nature of the hero emerges on as grand a scale as the tragic horror it provokes.

The duel itself proceeds realistically.[2] The build-up and the actual catastrophe are as overwhelming as the way it ends in the fourth section. The cold hand of death paralyzes all action. Nowhere else in the history of opera has this mood been so concisely and yet so movingly expressed. Everything combines to achieve the effect, the key of F minor and its subdominant, the three low male voices, the heavy chords on horns and bassoons and the deep register of the strings with their convulsive triplet figure.[3]

---

[1] Evidently he only draws his sword in the whirring demi-semiquaver passage in the violins after his first few words.

[2] Compare the forceful octave leaps in the violins with the smaller intervals in the bass. The portrayal in Gluck's ballet is similar. In both cases the model is probably French.

[3] Even this goes no higher than c'' (at the very end).

As the Commendatore with his broken melody slowly dies, Don Giovanni is torn between his inborn ruthless will to live and the awe which death inspires even in him (in this he differs from many of his precursors) — though again this must not be seen as a sign of pity or remorse.[1] Leporello, in common terror, utters two fearful cries after which he can only stammer. At the end flutes and oboes intone that soft elegiac melody, characteristic of Mozart in its chromaticism, which like a vigil by the dead body concludes the whole scene in a way quite unforgettable for the listener. This ending, however, turns quite surprisingly into a recitative which, after what has happened before, sounds truly 'secco' even in its expression. This odd second scene, in contrast to the usual secco recitative, pursues a definite dramatic idea. It is the first time Don Giovanni breaks loose from the preceding spell (he still has to sing sotto voce). His reawakened desire for action is directed first at Leporello, who is reprimanded and even threatened with a beating, but still cannot abstain from ironically preaching morals to his master. Finally they both disappear into the dark. The Introduction has rightly been praised as a model of dramatic exposition in opera. It is indeed a masterpiece of planning and execution. But its significance goes much further. Without Don Giovanni saying one word about himself, it gives a picture of his nature and of the forces which rule it that is unsurpassable; it presents him straight away in impassioned conflict with the supreme powers of life on earth. For this single incident, as the listener senses at once, it typical of his whole previous life. This scene and its premises have also been the subject of all too many romantic interpretations. The best known is E.T.A. Hoffmann's theory, still held by many to this day, that Donna Anna had been seduced by Don Giovanni.[2] Neither da Ponte nor his model Bertati say a single word to this effect; and above all it would run counter to the practice of the opera buffa to give the spectator only a hint of such an important occurrence. Opera

---

[1] The melodic similarity between his first few notes and Donna Anna's preceding 'Come furia disperata' is probably accidental. Gazzaniga elaborated this section far more extensively.

[2] Individual singers, like Mmes Bethman and Schröder-Devrient, agreed with this view.

buffa likes to be definite, the bolder the better; and particularly if it were a question of a maiden losing her honour, it would have presented the matter with complete frankness and certainly not in the manner of the romantic Hoffmann. To derive complex problems from the psychology of sex is absolutely alien to its nature. It presents unadorned natural instincts, and never considers the moral consequences of satisfying them. Don Giovanni would have been admired as the victorious male; but for his victim, on the other hand, a duped 'poverina', neither the poet nor his Italian audience would have mustered an ounce of sympathy; and with what commentary the comic servant would have accompanied the proceedings the connoisseur of this species can easily imagine.

Bearing this in mind, all Hoffmann's other hypotheses fall to the ground: first of all Donna Anna's continuing hypocrisy towards her unloved bridegroom Ottavio (which is refuted by da Ponte's text) and her secret love for Don Giovanni — which provoked Hoffmann to speak of her 'noble and tragic devotion'. The same applies to his view of Don Giovanni's character — that he tries to satisfy his yearning for the supernatural in love until, satiated in the end, he comes to despise the world, and in his scorn for God and nature no longer wants to enjoy women but only to corrupt them. It is characteristic of the 19th century with its predilection for erotic problems, that something of this kind should be brought into the relationship between Donna Anna and Don Giovanni at any price. Bertati and da Ponte never even hint at such a secret love on the part of Donna Anna; had they attached any value to the idea they would hardly have missed the opportunity of making the 'nascosa fiamma' the subject of an aria or at least a cavatina.

But above all, Mozart's music never even implies it. For him, Donna Anna is the daughter of a distinguished nobleman, an aristocratic character who, in contrast to Elvira, a woman completely possessed by passion, has all her feelings under control. No wonder this noble lady is deeply shocked by the death of her father, quite apart from filial affection; she feels his wounds as if they were her own. The image of blood that the murdered man at first impresses on her mind is like the vision of a madwoman, so unthinkable is the very idea for her. But when this first storm has passed her reaction becomes more clear-cut. The attempt on her honour pales completely before the memory of the deed itself. She certainly is under the spell of Don Giovanni, but for her he is not a seducer, but a savage master who in his unbridled impulsiveness has set himself up as the authority over life and death. Her hatred for this man, who in murdering her father has also delivered her a mortal blow, overpowers all her sensual emotions. This hatred is not, therefore, a concealed form of love, as it is with Elvira; it is not a self-tormenting call for the return of former bliss, but for the blood of the offender, anxious to continue the game of life and death that he himself began. This is the only way in which Donna Anna reacts to Don Giovanni's eruption into her life. Moreover, she does not behave at all like an Armida, thirsting for revenge, and it is therefore quite wrong to give the part to a dramatic soprano,[1] for Mozart conceived her as a young girl whose strength of character is tempered with virginal tenderness and modesty. In contrast to Elvira, who always acts independently, she never takes the initiative but leaves that to Don Ottavio. That he is inadequate vis-à-vis Don Giovanni is part of her destiny, although she is unaware of this. As to her love for Don Ottavio, neither da Ponte nor Mozart have the slightest doubt of it, only her love is not like that of Elvira or Zerlina. It is based not on sensuality, but on ethical precepts, as indeed is her whole being. In this way Mozart introduces a moral law into his drama, acknowledging it as one of the realities of the universe. So this stern and noble figure, Mozart's very own creation, takes her place in the opera, contrasting strongly with the rest of the characters but moving towards the same goal as all the other forces that influence the course of the drama.

For many different forces are at work here. Don Giovanni's daemonism runs wild not only in sex but in all aspects of the life of the senses; it releases not only love but all the energies that are at work in human existence. From this point of view, Donna Anna also has her place in the drama without being involved in the frenzy of love that Don Giovanni unleashes. All those later interpretations only show the almost unlimited potentialities of the subject; they have nothing to do with Mozart's work.

[1] The originator of this practice was Mme Schröder-Devrient, who first sang Anna and not Elvira.

Donna Anna returns with Don Ottavio and finds her father slain. Mozart's mastery has fashioned what follows into a musically great scene. It combines recitativo accompagnato with free melodic writing, and with a dramatic flexibility that without Gluck's example might not have been possible. Horror is expressed first in the very Mozartian orchestral introduction which is short and impetuous. Notice the declamatory tone here: horrified, all Donna Anna sees at first is a dead body, then after another outburst in the orchestra (now in F minor) she recognizes it to be her father and almost breathless her voice races up the C major triad.[1] She relapses into boundless grief to the accompaniment of a touching passage for wind. Four times they intone their moving lament and each time she whispers it after them, a fifth lower and in shorter note-values; the last time they are joined by the strings with over-whelming affect.[2] Sorrowfully she seeks in vain for a sign of life (in a lovely wind passage over tremolo strings) and the mood then becomes tortured, the violins descending like grave shadows. Donna Anna faints away.

And now it is worth noticing the complete change of mood when Ottavio enters: both the voice part and the orchestra have short, disjointed phrases and here, too, the tension increases feverishly[3] till Donna Anna recovers. In contrast to Don Giovanni, the man of action, Don Ottavio shows himself from the beginning to be impulsive but weak-minded and sanguine, full of the best intentions but lacking the strength to carry them out; he is a man who looks on and comments but never acts. His affection for Donna Anna, however, which comes out in the last section, is touching.

The 'Duetto' that follows immediately is a classic example of Mozart's inspired freedom in his treatment of this form. It consists of two large sections separated by a recitative, to which the second section often refers. The construction of the first section is equally free. It begins with Donna Anna thinking that she sees her father's murderer instead of Don Ottavio. She sings wildly (in D

---

[1] It is significant that throughout the scene she stresses the first of the two frequently repeated words 'mio padre!'

[2] Notice the 'sharp' keys which rise eventually to an ardent F sharp major.

[3] At 'Cercatemi, recatemi qualche odor', Mozart uses Gluck's effective device of making the bass rise chromatically with sequences above it.

minor!) with a rhythm as hard as steel,[1] reminiscent of Gluck. But already in the the sixth bar the vocal line dissolves into disconnected phrases and the daughter's grief now has the upper hand for some time. The orchestra takes the lead, but only to paint once more a picture of utter despair with the restless second violin figures and the off-beat crotchets in the first violins and violas. Ottavio's consoling words sound sincere and beautiful against this background, at first also halting with emotion, but then settling into a warm cantilena;[2] no less convincing is Donna Anna's reply as she recovers from her delusion, to music that utterly refutes the idea of the unloved bridegroom. At his comforting words her frenzied despair softens and turns into truly feminine grief, though the orchestra clings to the same theme, and even intensifies its expression of suffering. Now Ottavio himself conjures up the old shadow again. His words 'Lascia, o cara, la rimembranza amara' recall the hard rhythm of the beginning (a deeply poetic move), but only to drive away the dreadful vision; even before he can present his 'hai sposo e padre in me' there is a sound of affecting consolation from oboes and bassoons:

This sort of woodwind writing is entirely Mozartian; nothing comparable has been devised by any Italian! The contrast in Ottavio's words could not have been worked out more succinctly; one need only notice the harmonies and the melodic line which is first declamatory and then beautifully lyrical. To deepen the effect of this sharp contrast, Mozart repeats the section. Then Donna Anna takes courage in the well-known scale motif for tremolo strings which clearly points towards the subsequent 'che giuramento, o Dei!', and in a short and forceful recitative exacts an oath from Ottavio. It is significant that the music of his oath lays more stress on 'occhi tuoi' and 'nostro amor' than on the prospective vengeance. If he had had a definite will of his own Mozart would have made him swear in more vigorous terms.

The second section of the duet is in two parts with an extended coda. It has more emotional content than just a furious vengeful outburst, as is usually understood. Even the text makes this clear;

---

[1] Especially noteworthy are the strong upbeats on 'Fuggi' and 'Lascia'

[2] The gradual transition to F major is beautifully effective here.

its describes in fairly conventional words that are reminiscent of Metastasio[1] the horror they both feel at being compelled to take this oath, and the tragedy into which they have suddenly been plunged. This daemonic awakening of primitive human instincts also dominates the music. Once more we hear the opera's fierce and grandiose opening, drawing the two of them into its mad turmoil.

At the very beginning this sinister motif appears:

imitated by the woodwind like an echo from an abyss,[2] while the effect is emphasized by the pedal A against which the outcry on 'cento' stands out all the more harshly. It is quite natural that in such a turmoil of emotions individual treatment of character is no longer possible. Both are drawn into the vortex together, and even Ottavio's oath now sounds not heroic but tormented and anxious, through the accompaniment of chromatic thirds. In the coda Mozart finally illustrates 'ondeggiar' and describes the flood of excitement, sometimes in wild, melismatic quavers,[3] sometimes in tugging syncopations that seem to make the earth tremble; the voices, which in the coda occasionally imitate each other to enhance the effect, have difficulty in holding their own against all this. The fury continues right through to the two final bars with their stubborn semiquaver figure.

The scene changes and Donna Elvira enters. We already know her from Molière; but as the figure of the sposa abbandonata she is also familiar to opera buffa. However, the latter always sides with the man and presents the woman as a dupe, as is still evident in Bertati's and Gazzaniga's first aria for Elvira, 'Povera femmina'. The 19th century tried to make Elvira's previous history more res-

---

[1] Compare the aria from *Artaserse*, 'Fra cento affanni e cento' (K.88)

[2] The subsequent ♩♩♩♩♩♩ only represents a large extension of the upbeat crotchet.

[3] One need only compare these 'coloraturas' with those of the Neopolitan composers to appreciate the enormous difference. The sharp clash of a semitone is in itself characteristic.

pectable,[1] but in vain; she is simply, as the libretto says, 'abbandonata da Don Giovanni', and so in the same position as many others. At the same time she is a passionate woman whose love for Don Giovanni is not merely a passing episode but the decisive experience of her life. She is of all the women in the opera the one who in her whole being is closest to Don Giovanni. His love has kindled in her a spark of the same consuming passion that burns in him. But whereas he, being the man, is constantly lured by a sensuous desire for new adventures, she can find the fulfilment of her longing only in him. Her aim is therefore not to be revenged but to win back Don Giovanni's love; this is always apparent even in her fiercest outbursts of hatred. And even when she has to recognize the hopelessness of her quest she strives to save her beloved from the fatal consequences of his actions. Therefore she returns at the end neither as a pious 'sister' to win his soul for Heaven, nor, like Gretchen, to bring about his 'salvation', a thought far from Mozart's mind; she simply wants to save the man she loves from annihilation.

In her first aria (No. 3), in which Don Giovanni and Leporello throw in short remarks in the buffo manner without affecting its progress in any way, this character of hers is at once clearly established. The solemn pathos of the key of E flat is in itself significant, as is the extensive ritornello which just by its sudden dynamic contrasts points to her inner agitation. In addition there is a succession of motifs[2] which, though very different from one another, have their origin in the same conception and illuminate various facets in turn. None of them takes precedence over the others; her deeply stirred emotions appear now as injured pride, now as defiant questioning of her fate, finally changing to a deceptively gentle mood, in which she takes up a familiar and delicate

---

[1] Gugler and Wolzogen assert that she has been fooled by Don Giovanni into a mock marriage and therefore is 'legally his wife'. Bulthaupt rightly rejects this impossible idea. But also the promise of marriage presupposed by Jahn is, if it means a bourgeois engagement, an unhappy notion. The meaning of 'sposa' in opera buffa is altogether very flexible; it does not necessarily describe a real 'bride'. See C. Adelmann, 'Donna Elvira as an artistic ideal and her embodiment at the Munich Hofbühne' (Munich 1888).

[2] The opening is reminiscent of Grétry.

Neapolitan motif with its interval of a fourth; all anger and hatred is for her, in the end, only disappointed love.[1] So this time it is the voice that adds the finishing touches to the portrait. But the orchestra again whips up her passion with its provocative upbeat and the syncopation of its second theme. Here the voice seems at first somewhat resigned; only at the words 'vo' farne orrendo scempio' does her hatred explode,[2] to express defiance almost in the style of opera seria. And it is at this particular moment that Mozart brings the other two characters into play. The effect is strikingly realistic; at first Don Giovanni pretends to sympathize with her, but then his old urge to seduce comes to the surface, notably in the monotonous whispering of the orchestral figure:

This already holds a dangerously sensuous charm; no wonder that just here Leporello comments on his master's words in his own way, half amused, half regretful. At the recapitulation, Elvira's temperament overflows in an extensive coloratura based on the triad of E flat, provoking in its turn a burst of triumph in the full orchestra. Again we hear, but now in a higher position and with a crescendo, that sweet, rocking motif in the violins, against which Don Giovanni sings, in the most affecting manner, his 'signorina!'. Once more the action is continued unexpectedly in secco recitative; Elvira's reproaches are left to this genuinely buffo device.

It is in the good old Italian tradition that after her violent rejection, this poor abandoned woman should be exposed to the jests of the comic character. From de Villiers onwards the catalogue of Don Giovanni's loves plays an important part; it seems to have been extremely popular since it was also incorporated into

---

[1] In this aria, for the first time in the opera, Mozart uses clarinets.

[2] The Italians had already carried over the use of large intervals from opera seria to opera buffa. In Traetta's *Cavaliere errante* Arsinda sings:

traf - fig - ge-rò quel se - no   se giun - gi a qual-che eccess-so

and Carrado in Piccinni's *Sposalizio di Don Pomponio* has:

e qua - le sa - ra ma - i   se que - sto n'è do - lor

other texts[1]. Bertati ends the scene with a duet between Pasquariello and Elvira, to stress the contrasts in the situation in true buffo style: da Ponte, however, though he follows his model pretty closely − particularly in this scene − lets Leporello speak by himself, perhaps at Mozart's prompting.

For the composer in this aria was aiming at quite different things from Gazzaniga in his duet. Admittedly it has often been considered a weakness that after such humiliation Elvira does not express herself in an aria, and Rochlitz has even suggested inserting here 'Mi tradì quell' alma ingrata', which was written later on for the second act − an unhappy idea, since the emotional content of this piece would entirely misrepresent Elvira's character from the start. But is her humiliation by Leporello really so painful? The injury already inflicted on her by Don Giovanni is complete; can she still feel insulted by the effusions of this rogue, to whom she was already hardly listening in the recitative? Let him chatter away; the injustice that his master has done can never be matched by his mocking words. If anything makes an impression on her it is not Leporello's derision, but the image of Don Giovanni that shines clearly even through this distortion. And so we come to the essential dramatic significance of this famous piece; it pictures Don Giovanni's character as seen through the eyes of his servant, who in one way is so much like him and in another so deeply rooted in the everyday. There is just enough in it to give us a convincing impression of the elemental force that inhabits Don Giovanni, and yet to make us smile at the impression it leaves on a smaller mind. So Don Giovanni is present once again in this aria, if only from a different perspective. All three numbers thus combine to give a grandiose outline of the hero's character.

This dramatic conception explains not only the character of the music but also the unusual form, where a quick movement is followed by a slow one instead of the reverse.[2] For the quick part brilliantly illustrates man's natural sensual instincts; every note seems to sparkle as Leporello becomes more and more involved in

---

[1] In Piccinni's *Incostante* the lover disowns his beloved, upon which the servant remarks to the jilted girl: 'nel suo catalogo dove tien registrate tutte l'innamorate, questa Giulia non vè.'

[2] Paisiello had already made use of this procedure.

its breathless excitement. But the second part is even more relevant for Leporello's character since it is more tangible and therefore of greater significance to him; it describes his master's outward appearance which arouses both his envy and his admiration: his cavalier nature, depicted by an aristocratic minuet, and his magic power over the most diverse kinds of women are illuminated by the colourful humour of Leporello's rascally mind, which only understands those aspects of a nobler spirit that correspond to his own nature.

The Allegro is freely cast in two sections. Its main characteristic is the fluttering quaver movement which stops only once, at the now proverbial 'Ma in Ispagna mille e tre' – the only place where light declamation gives way to sustained singing. In all this brilliance the wind play a picturesque role – the grace notes in the flutes (which seem to depict Leporello turning over each new page), followed by the oboes and horns expressing happy approval. The heroic flourish on the full orchestra after 'mille e tre' has a similar effect. As there are no modulations at all in this first section, the sudden move now into A major is all the more striking. It affects everything; the whole melodic line surges upwards, accompanied by a glittering concertino of flutes and horns against oboes and bassoons, until the almost brutal 'd'ogni forma, d'ogni età'. Then even the cellos and basses are drawn into this extraordinary succession of scales accompanied by ever-changing combinations of wind instruments, until finally the voice has its turn. One sees how Don Giovanni's temperament infects his servant more and more, until in the end he adopts an air of complete triumph, as though he himself had been the hero of all these adventures.

But the concluding dominant harmony leads us to expect something new, and now comes the figure of the man from whom all this strange power emanates: Don Giovanni in his outward appearance. Leporello's description of the perfect cavalier opens naturally to the strains of a minuet, in a measured, sculptured, melodic line. Again Mozart uses a free binary form. The beginning is anything but original, being a well-known type of Italian melody; but it becomes more and more so as it develops. Leporello knows his master extremely well; he knows that his ability to adapt himself to the ways of different women is his most dangerous weapon. So he describes the 'costanza' of the brunettes and the 'dolcezza' of the fair ones; while the 'stout' and the 'slender' ones, to whom the text gives no particular attributes, are all depicted by the same motif which returns later on reinforced by a trill, and with its fivefold repetition dramatically portrays the way Don Giovanni also makes no distinctions.

On the other hand, the idea of the 'large' and the 'small' ones, the most simple of all antitheses, fires Leporello's pictorial imagination again. Here it becomes quite clear that in describing his master he is using his own scale of comparison: this is as crude as his own behaviour would be in the same situation. The difference is well illustrated: with the 'large' woman everything moves gradually upwards, as does Leporello's part in long note-values until he reaches his high D with horn fanfares and powerful tutti chords; but then 'la piccina' descends again in a swift parlando. Neither effect can be described in words, and in any case they are quite unthinkable without lively Italian gesticulations. Finally 'la piccina' comes to rest on a pedal A, which introduces the second section.

Already by the eighth bar the music has diverged significantly, an interrupted cadence leading to B flat major. Here Leporello suddenly takes on a mysterious air; in fact his whispering conjures up all the daemonism of his master, though still with a tinge of the ordinary that one always has to expect from him. This time it lies in the unexpected appearance of a staccato figure in the bassoon, a sound that has an unmistakable symbolic effect.[1] Given Leporello's nature, common lechery was bound to play its part sooner or later in his account of sensual impulses; it is almost as if he were nudging Elvira suggestively with his elbow. The bassoon theme returns at the end of this section. The coda appeals to Elvira half compassionately, half tauntingly while the wind again take up and reinforce Leporello's vulgarity. Its climax comes in the syncopated coloratura:

quel che fa

---

[1] Mozart may have remembered the duet between Rosina and Barbole in Paisiello's *Barbiere*, where there is a similar sequence of chords with staccato notes for the bassoon, although there the intention is purely humorous.

whose insolence appears quite infamous if correctly performed.[1] Leporello departs in triumph, though not without paying Elvira a grotesque compliment. She, however, takes no more notice of his words than before. She only listens because the subject is Don Giovanni — this fellow's view of him and his own importunities leave her quite unconcerned. There is no need for her to reply. An angrily indignant aria at this point would only weaken the effect of the earlier numbers. So Elvira leaves the scene after a short secco recitative.

Clearly da Ponte sets out at the beginning of the opera to present effective sketches of all Don Giovanni's antagonists one after another, so we now move on to the rustic wedding party of Masetto and Zerlina. The form of its music — solo verses interspersed with choral refrains — is based on French models, whereas the mode of expression is Italian.[2] Its folk-music character is maintained by passages of almost continuous thirds and sixths, as well as bagpipe effects and solid unisons at the end of each refrain. Yet this is no ordinary folk-music as is shown by the three-bar phrase at the very beginning, whose figure B-C-D, repeated four times, is somehow provocative and agitating. The variants in Masetto's verse are also worth noticing, particularly in respect of the harmony.[3]

Now Masetto is separated from his Zerlina, much to his secret anger. His aria (No. 6) strikingly reflects his mood. Its principal theme is in the buffo style; the horn fanfare sounds like an imperious gesture from Don Giovanni that the simple fellow must instinctively obey whether he will or no — it is not for nothing that this theme returns again and again. He would indeed like to show Don Giovanni that he can see through him and make him the object of his mockery, but face to face with a cavalier he simply does not manage it. His mockery turns to agitated bitterness, and in the subsidiary theme ('cavalier voi siete già') with its cutting false relation, his grief breaks out quite openly, punctuated with furious asides to Zerlina. But the expression

[1] Lablache sang it, according to Jahn, somewhat nasally and with a sidelong glance at Elvira. This is no doubt on the right lines: but in any event the part of Leporello requires both an actor and a singer.

[2] Like Masetto's aria (No. 6) this piece is written on a separate sheet, which does not, however, imply a later insertion, but rather a revision during rehearsals in Prague.

[3] His verse is also one bar longer than Zerlina's.

becomes quite grotesque with the unison motif that suddenly dances in at the words 'faccia il nostro cavaliero cavaliera ancora te'; and this idea eventually so sours him that in the coda with its obstinate syncopations he has no idea where to stop. As if jeering at him, the orchestra once more breaks out with the 'cavaliera' theme,[1] and so even this secondary figure is firmly characterized.

It is not by accident that the Duettino 'Là ci darem la mano' (No. 7) has won such immense popularity. It fulfils its dramatic purpose with such ingenious lightness and naturalness that the whole improbable situation is forgotten. But first one must be clear about the character of Zerlina. She is neither coquettish and already slightly corrupted, as many singers seem to think, nor one of those village beauties who were the delight of our romantic grandmothers in their novel-reading. Her 'charming innocence' should also be treated with caution. There is nothing in Zerlina of the rustic belles of Rousseau's period, who were presented as the antithesis of debauched townswomen in popular operas. Neither is she a buffo caricature like Bertati's Maturina, but simply an unspoiled peasant girl with a lively temperament, natural grace and, above all, strong, healthy instincts. These govern all her feelings and actions, which are therefore not capable of analysis on an ethical plane dealing with innocence and guilt; and it is this naively sensual impulse that makes her fall into Don Giovanni's trap, and then return to Masetto. Mozart has freed this natural, subconscious instinct from all wordly codes and thus made it artistically viable, shaping events according to his higher ideas of realism and so silencing all reservations of either a moral or a dramaturgical kind.

That Don Giovanni will have an easy time here is clear from the beginning; but the way in which the two characters approach each other still remains a masterpiece of dramatic psychology. He knows that it is his being a nobleman that will most impress the

---

[1] Compare, by the way, the two following passages from Biagio's aria, in Gazzaniga:

peasant girl; he therefore chooses a courtly manner of speech, as if he were addressing an equal. But far more important is the peculiar warmth and suppressed urgency behind this courtship; consider, for instance, the very telling step of a fourth in the second bar, which one need only replace by one of the usual formulas, such as a sighing motif, to appreciate its full impact. That Don Giovanni is at first effective simply by the power of his singing is also significant; only at the end of each phrase do the wind instruments seem to sound like someone breathing deeply and heavily.

No wonder Zerlina repeats these enticing sounds as if under a spell – an inspired, poetical way of using Scarlatti's old duet form – and in the end develops them even further, in a state of strange excitement. The whole is illuminated by the seductive fervour of Mozart's A major music.[1] Now Don Giovanni follows up his attack in the more intense key of E major, supported by the wind in an expansive, glowing melodic style; her reply is a touching, though brief, thought for poor Masetto.[2] But soon afterwards she is fluttering with a restless little tune like a captive bird in a net. With uncanny assurance and without undue haste, Don Giovanni closes the trap; he starts again from the beginning. But this time Zerlina has come to the point where she takes his phrases straight from his mouth. It is also interesting that he is joined by a flute[3] and she by a bassoon, until on the words 'Partiam ben mio da qui', he draws all three woodwind instruments[4] to his side in double octaves. Zerlina's singing becomes more and more fervent while a strange power seems to emanate from Don Giovanni's short phrases. His last 'andiam' brings him victory, as expected.

In the second part of the Duettino Don Giovanni, now sure of his victim, descends to her rustic level, to gain her submission by the use of his most deadly weapon (see above). That is the meaning of this pastoral movement, from the pedal note at the beginning with its comfortably rocking impression of bliss, to the joyful

---

[1] See also the Terzetto (no. 16), the only other A major piece in the opera.

[2] The figure in the violins is also a half-jesting reminder of Masetto.

[3] The flute plays a characteristic part in Don Giovanni's music, as can be seen throughout the opera.

[4] Flute, oboe, bassoon.

tripping of the conclusion.[1] It is all imagined from Zerlina's standpoint, just as the Andante is seen from Don Giovanni's. Some have demanded more fire and passion, but this would be to misjudge Don Giovanni's position. For him this conquest is nothing out of the ordinary; only an amusing pastime that involves no effort on his part. Nor does Zerlina find it dramatic; she has simply followed her natural instinct, and now that it looks like being gratified she enjoys it with all the uncomplicated, warm impulsiveness of her nature. So this happy idyll comes to pass, and its rustic character adds a piquant attraction for the seducer. How much more arresting is the effect of this scene, in the form of a duet, than if Don Giovanni were first to declare his affection for Zerlina in an aria and she to reply with another, only then to be followed by a duet to conclude the scene!

Elvira intercepts the deluded Zerlina. Her aria (No. 8) is written in a curious, archaic style.[2] Equally old-fashioned are the concentrated ternary form (although admittedly the third part is very varied and extended), the sequence of modulations to E and B minor in the middle section, the austere orchestration over an antiquated type of bass which recalls earlier ground bass compositions, the weighty cadences reminiscent of Handel, for example, and most of all the taut, relentless tread of the dotted rhythm. All this distinguishes the aria fundamentally from Mozart's usual manner of arousing the most diverse feelings with a few strokes of his pen. Here there is a striking uniformity, which leaves room for only one independent orchestral interlude, and that soon after the beginning; the whole piece is like one powerful wave of temperament that swells continually and finally breaks in the wild coloratura on 'fallace'.

This aria is certainly not supposed to be a moral sermon aimed at Zerlina; such an idea would be quite un-Mozartian. The composer, it is true, wants to create a sharp contrast with the gentle, sensuous atmosphere of what has gone before, and therefore accumulates as much austerity and harshness as he can muster.

---

[1] It has no tempo mark in the original score. Indeed there is no need for one, as the change of time signature and the general character of the music are quite sufficient to produce the enhanced effect.

[2] Mozart's alleged heading 'Nello stile di Handel' is pure invention.

That was his main reason for reverting to an archaic style. But anything didactic is far from Elvira's mind; despite a few words in the text to that effect, it all evaporates in face of the indignation she feels at the sight of the amorous couple. Leporello's mockery she could ignore, but now, when she surprises her former lover in the act, her passion knows no bounds. For frenzied passion is the essential keynote of this aria, and it is directed much less at Zerlina than at Don Giovanni. Elvira must destroy this idyll, not out of hatred or even pity for her rival, who is of no interest whatever to her, but simply out of fury at Don Giovanni's excessive avidity.

She succeeds in robbing him of his prey for the time being, and now Donna Anna and Don Ottavio enter, searching for the murderer of the Commendatore. Don Giovanni, who despite all setbacks is once again master of the situation, promises with perfect chivalry to help them; he even draws near to Donna Anna, with assurances of sympathy. At this point Elvira intervenes once again, preparing the ground for the Quartet (No. 9), which comes at a moment (very much in Mozart's style) when all the participants find themselves faced with a completely new situation. Anna and Ottavio are bewildered by Elvira's intervention; Elvira attempts to unmask Don Giovanni who, for his part, tries every trick he can think of to get her out of the way. The Quartet is constructed as a three-part cycle; the middle part, however, unlike that of the previous aria, is by far the longest, and falls into several independent sections which have only one thing in common: that they all revolve round the dominant of B flat major and avoid the principal key. Only at the end does the latter assert itself again with full effect.

The first entry of the main theme is particularly fine. Elvira begins, not as explosively as before with Zerlina, but still only controlling her emotion with difficulty[1] all the way up the melancholy final phrase:

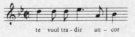

te   vuol tra - dir   an - cor

---

[1] The whole first bar is a strong up beat, and the 'Non' on a note lasting three beats has the same violent accent as the 'fuggi' in the first duet of the opera.

This now becomes the motif of the whole piece, ranging through all the vocal and orchestral parts and finally turning against Don Giovanni himself. The pity that Elvira was unable to feel for Zerlina now overcomes her on Donna Anna's behalf. But even more, this touching melody becomes, as it were, the mournful voice of all womanhood trampled underfoot by Don Giovanni, constantly reminding us of the text at its first appearance. First it rises in the orchestra over the violins and clarinets up to the flutes, to be taken up by Anna and Ottavio, who are musically inseparable throughout the piece and whose grief arouses the compassion of the noble Elvira. Even Don Giovanni has this refrain, though he tries to render the whole situation ridiculous by asserting that Elvira is out of her mind. Thus the theme on his lips assumes an ironical and aristocratically condescending air; the orchestra, however, stubbornly repeats the original version.

Elvira's agitation now becomes all the more intense; she assumes the lead more vigorously, expressing her anger with ever changing melodic outlines and compelling Don Giovanni to follow her. The more the argument between them grows, the stronger becomes the tension for the other two. It descends on them all like a dark cloud, from which Elvira's angry phrases shoot out like flames. Clearly Don Giovanni, driven more and more into a corner, in the end prefers direct negotiation with Elvira; in short semiquavers — accompanied by the orchestra in unison — which openly betray his concern, he whispers his 'siate un poco più prudente' to her. This is no buffo patter but grim, barely suppressed anger at her stubbornness. All he achieves, however, is that Elvira answers him in the same angry tone, but out loud. Of course it is just this excited argument that increases the suspicion of the other two; the beginning returns with that refrain-like theme ('te vuol tradir ancor') and finally turns Donna Anna's suspicions into certainty.

In the recitative of the next scene (No. 10) there is a gloomy sound in the bass, followed by a shrill outburst from the full orchestra — including the trumpets. Its cutting, accentuated dissonances and unyielding rhythms recall the terrible image of the previous night to which Donna Anna's mind returns again and again in this scene.[1] It is a study in the most varied types of

---

[1] The C minor phrase in the wind: is already familiar from the first movement of the C minor Piano Sonata, K. 457.

recitative writing. First comes a C minor section of intense pathos with almost hectic alternation between voice and instruments. The bass line is broad and emphatic and the vocal part strongly declamatory, spanning wide intervals. Then follow seven bars of pure secco all on the same harmony, whispered rapidly in a tone of the utmost secrecy. Now Donna Anna begins the actual narration, which starts in the dark key of E flat minor and makes full use of its sombre effect. There is a compelling atmosphere in this opening, and at the mention of the unknown intruder the harmony changes with convincing effect to B minor. But then as Donna Anna describes the actual assault, the orchestra in a violent stringendo[1] reverts to the opening theme,[2] which is followed at once by a sinister silence. The stillness is interrupted only by a brutal forte chord. What effects might later composers have devised to depict this struggle! Mozart makes only slight, but unmistakable, allusions, like the tugging syncopation at 'svincolarmi, torcermi!' or the interrupted cadence in F at Ottavio's 'Ohimè! respiro!' where all the tension of the preceding bars is released in one sigh; he achieves his effects, as always, by dynamic contrasts. The conclusion is dominated by the savage opening theme, which appears once again with redoubled momentum, greatly extended cadences and, especially towards the end, a peculiar tension in its harmonies further increased by the repetition of the words 'compiè il misfatto'. Until the very last bar we have, in fact, no idea in which key this progression will end.

From this extreme tension springs the aria, a beautiful example of Mozart's ability to reduce old forms to the most economic proportions and to fill them with strong emotion. There are still traces of the old ternary form, no longer as a cliché, but rather as a natural vehicle for what has to be expressed. The verbosity of earlier composers is replaced by a conciseness of expression that says only what is essential. In its emotional content the aria paints a vivid portrait of Anna's character as described earlier on. Melodically the idiom of the opera seria is still evident, as is shown by the wide intervals in the opening cry of revenge and by the sighing character of the section that immediately follows ('che il padre mi

---

[1] Note her breathless declamation and the continual interruptions by the orchestra.
[2] Only for this main theme do the wind join in.

tolse'). But nowhere does it become mere theatre,[1] thanks chiefly to the highly original and significant orchestration, which by leaving out the more soft-toned woodwind (flutes and clarinets) gives an air of austerity to the whole.

Instead of the usual drum bass the aria begins with a restless throbbing in the upper strings; only then do the cellos and basses join in with their sombre and forceful motif, which is answered and extended by the woodwind. Such orchestral writing, as indeed in most parts of this opera, sounds like a phenomenon of nature, here like the rumbling of distant thunder. All the more does it ring true when, as Donna Anna expresses her grief, the orchestra unites most affectingly with the vocal line. Then, however, its powerful imitations come to the fore with renewed vigour. In the middle section we hear Anna once more in that sombre mood inspired by her visions, already evident in the first duet. Again the dreadful scene passes before her eyes accompanied by dark violas and bassoons; but it no longer inspires horror, only melancholy, and the end brings back that sighing motif into which Donna Anna, after proclaiming to the full her thoughts of vengeance and hate, pours all her grief for her father. The same mood appears once more in the third section, though at the memory of the terrible deed her feelings of vengeance mount even higher. In a few agitated bars this memory is also drawn into the stream of passion which floods the coda. The orchestral epilogue is very characteristic of Mozart, finally sinking down into piano as if exhausted after so much effort.

Now follows the absolute antithesis; Mozart, ever the great master of contrasts, continues with Don Giovanni's famous aria

---

[1] This is clear from the sketches. Donna Anna's characteristic theme:

Or sai chi l'o - no - re   ra - pir a me vol - se   chi fu il tra - di - to - re

originally looked like this:

Or sai chi l'o - no - re   ra - pir a me vol - se   chi fu il tra - di - to - re

The improvement lies not only in the declamation (how effective is the emphasis here on the most important words 'sai,' 'rapir' and 'fu'!) but also in the character of the melody: from a style of grand pathos, as in the opera seria, it is toned down to the emotional range of a deeply disturbed girl, whose real feelings become apparent in the following bars.

(No. 12). Don Giovanni is completely carried away by the thought of the approaching feast and the triumph it will bring him. Sensual expectation intoxicates him; even the dances to be performed, 'menuetto, follia, alemana', are already swirling in his head. And above all there is the new addition to his catalogue! So much for the text. An Italian buffo composer would certainly not have missed the opportunity for a little light-hearted devilry; even the rhythm chosen by Mozart was well known to the Italians. But their music, after all, only aimed at making the emotional state described in the text as clear as possible. With Mozart, on the other hand, we observe again the process that we know from certain parts of *Figaro*: his music not only describes or elucidates the emotion with more or less spirit — it represents, it is itself the emotion. We are immediately assailed by a torrent of passion whose unrestrained sensuality sweeps over us like a whirlwind. Here is something quite different from an ordinary aria, however passionate, and it explains the hold it has over our senses even today.

Its inherent driving force is its rhythm which, over a foundation of almost continuous quavers, constantly produces new melodic formulae, the pattern only slackening to allow longer notes for the triumphant cadences before each return of the main theme. The

rhythmic scheme   ♩ ♫ | ♩ ♩   does not consist of two

equally stressed bars; it is essential to regard the first as the upbeat, so that the main accent falls on the first crotchet of the second. Only then does the piece acquire the effervescent power that gives it its hallmark. The points at which this upbeat is lengthened by yet another crotchet are very characteristic — for instance at the second entry of 'Ch'il menuetto'. The effect is of a sudden intensification that is clearly connected with the chromatic descent that follows; and a similar thing happens at the passage beginning 'd'una decina devi aumentar'. These psychological points renew the excitement again and again; and the melody shows them too, especially in the little chromatic passages that give added expression in a most individual way. Otherwise it is all solidly diatonic; the main idea, for example, is based entirely on the notes of the major triad. A fascinating effect is achieved by the appearance of the minor key at 'Ed io frattanto': here speaks all the daemonism of a mastermind.

Not surprisingly, the piece is quite free in form, for all its breathtaking unity. It comes nearest to the rondo, since Don Giovanni, after all kinds of excursions, always comes back to the main theme. Mozart's skill ensures that each return is like another climax; it is also noteworthy that in the course of the aria he drives the voice higher and higher, right into the coda, by delaying the cadence again and again — in the old Italian way, but with striking psychological effect. Moreover, in the whole piece the voice only rests for two bars, in which the beginning of the principal theme rings out in the orchestra. This includes all the wind instruments except the trumpets, and apart from short episodes[1] they always appear together, with the exception of the flute, which together with the first violins doubles the vocal line, almost continuously, two octaves higher, and so considerably enhances the sensuous colour of the piece.[2] Characteristic, too, is the rich sound of the orchestra; at the very beginning, for instance, second violins and violas provide full four-part harmony.

Finally there are the dynamics; once again there are no gradual changes, but only sharp contrasts. It is the orchestra that provides the ecstatic forte and sforzato effects, lighting up the scene now in this, now in that quarter. But it never drowns the vocal line, and the singer must guard against trying to characterize his part by excessive vocal display. The melody and especially the rhythms of this aria must emanate not only from his throat but also from his whole appearance, from every look and every gesture. To this day there are few pieces in which the composer sets the performer such a difficult task.

In complete contrast to this piece, whose rhythm is its lifeblood, Zerlina's aria (No. 13) relies mainly on melodic devices. The object is to conciliate Masetto who is justifiably offended by her scene

---

[1] e.g: the provocative grace note in the woodwind at the first mention of the dances, at which point (here as well as later) the basses are also set in motion.
[2] See the duet (No. 7). In *Entführung* (No. 14) and *Zauberflöte* (No. 13) the piccolo is used to portray sensuality, admittedly with reference to characters like Osmin and Monostatos. It is significant that in 'Finch 'han dal vino' the clarinet is used only to influence the colour of the general sound, never as a solo instrument.

with Don Giovanni — a theme that was as familiar to the Italians as the view that in such cases a daughter of Eve is implicitly superior to a dim-witted man. The same goes, in Mozart, for Blondchen and Pedrillo and is even truer with Masetto and Zerlina, since she has already had her adventure with Don Giovanni. Even now she remains true to her character. There is no question of repentance or of sentimentality. Her adventure with a nobleman is as natural to her as the conviction that her relationship with Masetto, to whom she is in her own way as devoted as ever, cannot be affected in the long run. In the end the good-natured fellow will not be able to resist her, as she full well knows. After all, in her scene with Don Giovanni nothing bad actually happened; that this was not due to any restraint on her part does not greatly concern her. But that fact is enough to allow her to play the role of the wronged woman, and having thus made Masetto uncertain she then employs all the feminine techniques of flattery to beguile his senses.

This is certainly in her nature, but the way she proceeds shows clearly that she has learned a good deal from Don Giovanni. With a tender, bewitching charm she tries to ensnare him, with an ingenious mixture of genuine affection and shrewd calculation; it is as if Masetto were also subjected to the seductive spell to which she herself had succumbed in the scene with Don Giovanni. After all, the two pieces are identical in form and time signature; and in both cases the Andante and the Allegro have the relationship of courtship and fulfilment. With Zerlina, however, everything is touched on more lightly, in a more feminine way, although we can see that since her contact with Don Giovanni she has become fully conscious of her feminine powers. She certainly loves her Masetto, but she also enjoys letting him feel her superiority.

This basically simple situation, which the Singspiel with its provincial joviality had often depicted in detail, has been elaborated and transfigured by Mozart through the tenderness of his cantilena, that never falls into inappropriate pathos or false sentimentality. He keeps strictly to the idea of the child of nature, so that rhythm and harmony remain subsidiary to the melodic line, which itself is almost completely devoid of chromaticism and moves in diatonic or chordal intervals. The main theme of the two-part Andante is already typical with its descending phrases built in thirds; and the codetta is particularly effective with its top F not only marking the highest point in the melodic line but also triggering off a delightful rocking between tonic and dominant triads. Each phrase here has the effect of a new gesture: it is as if a gentle hand were caressing a cheek more and more affectionately.

The harmony in Zerlina's two arias is as simple as possible: tonic and dominant, nothing else; on the other hand, the orchestra clearly speaks a language of flattery and endearment. Zerlina's first theme is doubled by the strings and in the second phrase it is taken up by the woodwind, spanning three octaves. But above all the solo cello assumes the role of the courting lover throughout the aria. It surrounds every phrase of the vocal line, with its enticing figuration frequently suggesting two-part writing in disguise: a soft melodic lower part parallel with the voice, and an upper one remaining static on the fifth, C. Once, ('e le care tue manine') there is even an eloquent dialogue in imitation between voice and cello. In the recapitulation, which incidentally extends the first upbeat in the woodwind in a highly original way and strengthens its expressiveness by the syncopation in the oboes (the descending melodic line being thrown into particular relief), the melody is slightly varied and embellished; but now the violins begin an incessant trill, as if the whole crossfire of sly, amorous glances were bearing down on poor Masetto. Triumphantly Zerlina holds him under her spell through the little motif

and its different variants, and so wins an easy victory while the cello happily cavorts in demi-semiquavers.

From an extension of that motif there begins a new 6/8 section, which turns out to be nothing else than continued jubilation above the cello. It is a dance round the defeated Masetto, full of an innocently roguish feeling of triumph, now moving up and down in broken triads, now in exultant coloratura. Zerlina can hardly stop herself, swinging gracefully up to the fifth and down again till the orchestra, with the happily humming cello, brings the piece to an end. Zerlina's two arias are like rays of sunshine in the sombre, deeply emotional realm of this drama.

The first Finale cannot compare in a literary sense with its predecessor in *Figaro*. It does not grow in the same inevitable

way, nor does it develop the action consistently, but strings together various scenes, though with a skilful sense of climax. It is a
complex of final scenes planned with a good sense of continuity,
rather than an organically constructed finale; and the reason is
quite simply the sheer number of external events in the action.
But where da Ponte fell short Mozart succeeded completely. He
made the whole piece lead up to the climax: the ball. The festivities resound from the very start and become more and more
distinct between the various episodes. These, too, bear a close
relationship to it and raise our expectation higher and higher, each
according to its very different emotional content. Thus on entering the ballroom, despite all the festive gaiety, we already
find ourselves in the sultry atmosphere that usually precedes a
catastrophe.

The first section follows immediately after the last scene.
Zerlina hears Don Giovanni's voice from inside and at once falls
under his spell again. Naturally Masetto's suspicion is once more
aroused, while she tries in great agitation to prevent a clash. The
tense situation is made abundantly clear by the angry snarling of
the orchestra at the beginning and by the gloomy motifs in the
vocal line, such as the following:

which creeps again and again into all the orchestral parts. Excitedly
Zerlina's voice flutters round Masetto's grim little song, and in the
short middle section in G major, where he comes quite emphatic
with the crescendo in the trumpet motif:

she clings to his vocal phrases in great anxiety. At the return of
the opening music the tension is increased by every available
means. Masetto's trumpet theme appears this time more quietly in
the flutes:

and finally in utter desperation in the violins:

Now the ball is brought to our notice for the first time, in the
festive anapaestic rhythm that we know all too well from what
has gone before. Don Giovanni invites the rustic party to his

house and hastily gives last instructions to his servants. These repeat the invitation in a no less chivalrous manner; they have assimilated his noble manners well. Then the sound of the chorus gradually dies away,[1] leading to the next scene — the first really important episode in the Finale — which introduces changes of tempo, time signature and key.

We find ourselves again in that seductive atmosphere familiar from the Duettino (No. 7). First there is the mysterious beauty of the dialogue between strings and flutes; the somewhat uncertain tone in which Zerlina begins does not hide the fact that she is already on the point of falling a prey once again to Don Giovanni, and when he swiftly seizes her hand, accompanied by the whole orchestra, the old game is about to repeat itself. He begins by echoing all her phrases, but now he no longer needs to play the rustic lover, for Zerlina is already trembling with secret desire, and so he only has to emphasize her own bashfully stammered words. The situation is much more tense than in the Duettino, and almost explodes with longing[2] when the voices come together to the accompaniment of a semiquaver figure in the woodwind that ripples constantly downwards.

When we hear Zerlina's anxious fluttering semiquavers her resistance seems finally to be overcome and at that moment Masetto steps forward from his hiding place. The music that accompanies this surprise is a counterpart to that in *Figaro* where the Count suddenly finds Cherubino in the chair. There is no orchestral outburst, no change of time signature or tempo, not even a forte, but instead the music is frozen into one single motif that also brings about an unexpected modulation to D minor: with a further motionless figure on A in the horns, whose rhythm bears a suspicious resemblance to Masetto's trumpet motif mentioned above. This combination of ideas brings all progress to a halt, as if there were nothing more to expect; the

---

[1] A small point; but it is interesting to see how the violins' dotted rhythm, as the music gradually dies away, turns into a quaver figure six bars before the end, as if becoming more and more blurred.
[2] Don Giovanni's 'Vieni un poco' corresponds to Almaviva's 'Son venuti a vendicarmi' in the first Finale of *Figaro*; both express the triumph of a nobleman whose desire is at last fulfilled.

surprise paralyzes everyone and everything. With Don Giovanni, however, this does not last long. As if nothing had happened he conducts Zerlina to her Masetto, while the orchestra titters sarcastically. His last phrase, 'Non può più star senza di te', the foolish simpleton even stammers after him. But again the festivities are heard within (the same contre-danse[1] in which Don Giovanni later joins with Zerlina), and in the excitement the preceding upset is forgotten. An exhilarating little movement unites all three, as if they were transported by the sound of the dance music to a completely different sphere.

At that moment the merrymaking stops with a sudden jolt. In the woodwind something like a dark veil seems to descend, and the F major tonality gives way in the next section to D minor, a key which in this opera always has its own particular significance. This episode unites Elvira, Donna Anna and Ottavio, who have come to unmask Don Giovanni at his own festivity. They too are masked, and the orchestra, which harks back to the semiquavers of the previous scene, including individual turns of phrase, also tells us that they are in a state of suspense about the feast, but in their case for different reasons. Their masks conceal the feverish unrest that comes before a decisive action. The whole section never breaks away from minor keys (D and G minor) and the ever recurring rhythm increases the unease so that the F major of the next minuet will come to the listener as a relief. The melody also conforms to a type frequently to be found in Mozart's D minor pieces, dominating here the vocal as well as the instrumental parts:[2]

It is a subtle feature of this scene that before it is concentrated into a full ensemble Elvira leads and Don Ottavio follows her with the same music; while Donna Anna goes her own way, alone. She does this not in the same sense as at the beginning of her revenge aria, even though she is now coming much nearer her real aim in life, but because she foresees with true feminine intuition the decisive moment approaching and is, above all, anxious on behalf

---

[1] Except that the first two bars are missing, as with the march in *Figaro*.
[2] Compare this with the first duet in *Don Giovanni* ('Fuggi crudel'), and also with the beginning of the D minor Piano Concerto K 466. It appears again in the last movement of Beethoven's Piano Sonata Op. 31 No. 2.

of her bridegroom. This is shown by the bassoons' chromatic passages in sixths that introduce her first entry, and especially by her G minor episode. So all the feelings aroused by the critical moment ahead find expression with striking succinctness.

We now begin to hear the minuet (this time in F major) and the ball moves once more into the foreground. Against the dance tune Don Giovanni and Leporello engage in a lively dialogue, partly in parlando, while the others comment on their behaviour, leading up to Leporello's invitation to them all to join the dancing. The same procedure is found with the wedding march in *Figaro* and it has been imitated since in countless scenes. Here, too, individual features are clearly characterized, for example Don Giovanni's insolent 'dì che cì fanno onor', then Leporello's cry, beautifully true to life, and his chivalrous invitation to which Ottavio replies, also as a perfect nobleman. But no sooner has Leporello disappeared than the whole scene changes completely, starting with a short, terse orchestral motif that corresponds to the one before the D minor section. After all, this famous mask trio is basically the ideal continuation of that section; its unexpected entry and its profound effect are prepared by the masterly insertion of the little dance movement.

Mozart has shaped this scene, short though it is, so very differently from those around it that it almost becomes the central point of the whole Finale, or at any rate the nucleus of its 'internal action'. It occupies a similar position to the A major section of the quartet in *Entführung* which, incidentally, also begins with a solemn introduction. It is as if Mozart were drawing away the last veil from the inner lives of his characters and showing them to us in the light of a most exalted transfiguration. They seem suddenly to shed everything in them that is accidental, conditional or compulsive. In the D minor episode the closeness of the atmosphere weighed heavily on them all; but now that their antagonists have forced the decision on them, they lose their inhibitions and go purposefully and clearsightedly to meet their destiny. This is how Mozart conceived their prayer, to which he also gives a distinctly religious tone.

For the first time in this Finale the voices show their full expressive power. Their first phrase is a cappella, without any instrumental accompaniment, and thus the entry of the woodwind (the strings are still silent) has a quite striking effect. Donna Anna has found her confidence once more; but again hers is no wild cry of revenge: all that lies behind her. The more the drama progresses, the more unworldly, one might almost say ethereal, does the expression of her feelings grow, and the looser become the ties which bind her to this world of primitive passions and impulses. In the terzetto she sings with ardent eloquence; in an expansive melodic line her voice floats up and down, and the scale passages and small grace notes serve to enhance the impression of a confidence that springs from the bottom of her heart. In this piece too Ottavio is her faithful companion, but between them there rises the jagged melodic line of the much more passionate Elvira. It is she, not Anna, who openly expresses thoughts of retribution; towards the end, moreover, she has a phrase ('vendichi, vendichi il giusto ciel') reminiscent of Donna Anna's revenge aria. All the way through, her part goes its own way alongside that of the other two, coming in only when they reach the end of their phrases; and her entries usually raise the level of emotion, especially when she sails in on her top A flat.

The full sonority of the wind instruments (employed sparingly, however) throws a shining radiance over the whole; only in the seventh bar ('protegga il giusto ciel') does the first clarinet, supported by a staccato accompaniment in the bassoon, begin with a deep arpeggio figure in semiquavers which later blossoms into semiquaver triplets. This sonority has a completely original effect, and its dark colouring most effectively emphasizes the intensified repeat of the prayer. At the end the instruments take up Anna's last phrase.

The next scene takes us into the ballroom with all its activity, a familiar situation in Italian opera buffa.[1] The atmosphere is therefore also Italian: a whirling *brio* with festive noises punctuated by whispering and laughter. This is a picture of the bustle that comes with a break in the dancing. Coffee, chocolate and sorbets are passed round — in short, after the lofty heights of the trio we are once more in the midst of everyday life, this time in the luxurious, sensually stimulating atmosphere that surrounds Don Giovanni. Again it is the orchestra that sets the mood; voices

---

[1] In Piccinni's *Donne vendicate* the newcomers also express their thanks.

sometimes join in with short phrases and sometimes interrupt, usually in a light parlando. The lively picture unfolds in an entirely realistic way.

Only the jealous Masetto stands aside, watching; touchingly his 'Ah Zerlina, giudizio!' rings out twice, and in his brief duet with her an ominous crackling begins in the orchestra. Then the basses suddenly settle on a B flat for 14 bars: Don Giovanni again holds out his hand to Zerlina, and Leporello, who on such festive occasions is fond of playing the cavalier, follows his example with the other girls. Again the flutes, this time supported by the clarinets, are Don Giovanni's faithful attendants. But once more it is Masetto, though he is only able to stammer out odd, incoherent little phrases, who presents the main obstacle. Zerlina is already quite angry about this; but the other two, with the inimitable:[1]

Quel Ma - set - to mi par stra - lu - na - to, qui bi - sog - na cer - vel - lo a-do-prar

at once come to the conclusion that Masetto must be kept busy. In an excited repetition of the first part the action comes to an end.

So far the music has maintained a simple, rustic character for the benefit of the country folk. Now, at the entry of the three masks, it suddenly rises to an aristocratic level. Not only does the key change abruptly, but trumpets and timpani are added to the orchestra. It is an official, ceremonious reception of noble guests, for which many a distinguished home in Vienna may have provided Mozart with a model. Even Leporello, who functions here as the major-domo, begins his speech like a grand seigneur, and the gracious reply of the newcomers preserves the same air of nobility. With the amiability of a man of the world Don Giovanni repeats several times, 'e aperto a tutti quanti, viva la libertà', and this has sometimes, oddly enough, been made the occasion for unmotivated cheers for political liberty, echoed eventually by the chorus and even in some cases by the audience! But Don Giovanni, the aristocrat, would not take it into his head to demonstrate for political freedom. He means only the freedom conferred by

---

[1] It is distinctly reminiscent of Figaro's 'Non più andrai.'

wearing masks, and if his distinguished guests enter into the spirit of it all, it is out of formal courtesy towards their host; they would not wish to be inferior to him in social savoir-faire. However, the peasants at the ceremony have no idea of distinguished behaviour, and it is precisely for this reason that Mozart by presenting everything in faithful detail makes the scene one of such biting irony for the spectator, particularly the spectator of his day.

Now Don Giovanni gives the sign for the dance to begin again, and when it does, the dramatic tension that has been building up all this time finally breaks. Of all the ballroom scenes that opera can boast before[1] or since, Mozart's has never been surpassed, either dramatically or musically. Its central idea, the dance, is of a purely musical nature, but Mozart connects it at once with the dramatic element by combining three different dances. Thus Don Giovanni has the opportunity to divide up his guests and to avoid those he does not wish to see. His aristocratic guests begin a minuet, he himself joins with Zerlina in a contre-danse, and Masetto is dragged by Leporello into a dashing 'Teutscher'. Consequently there are also three orchestras playing. The nobility has the well-appointed house orchestra that Don Giovanni keeps like every respectable aristocrat in Vienna, whereas a pair of village bands playing in two parts, violins and basses, is enough for the peasants.[2] This tripartite arrangement, also reflected spatially, becomes the basis for the development of the action. The three dances are the main point of interest; the individual characters have to conform to them under all circumstances, so that detailed atmospheric description is excluded from the start.

---

[1] Two contemporary Italian examples are noteworthy: the second finale in Galuppi's *Partenza e ritorno die marinari* (1756), where the ballroom scene also opens with a minuet and the action progresses on the basis of this dance melody; and the first finale in Piccinni's *Viaggiatori* which is also built round a 'Tempo di Minuè'.

[2] The practice of using several orchestras was known to the Italians (such as Paisiello and Galuppi) as well as to Gluck. Wolzogen justifiably criticizes the idea of having the different dances completely separated on stage; he also attacks the arbitrary prolonging of this scene at the Paris Opera. This time Mozart does not introduce any national colouring like that of the Fandango in *Figaro*. Indeed the music for this feast would be more suitable for the mansion of an Austrian magnate than the country house of a Spanish nobleman.

The combination of three dances, completely different from one another both in character and in rhythm, is in itself a contrapuntal masterpiece. True, the equation : 2 3/4 bars = 3 2/4 bars is fundamentally simple, as is : one 3/8 bar = one crotchet divided into triplets. The consummate skill lies in combining the three dances in such a way that each retains its independent character, while their harmonious concurrence appears accidental. The entries, as each dance starts, are presented very realistically: both the small bands prepare themselves by tuning up. The open strings are checked, one experiments with pizzicato, another tries a little trill, another plucks all the strings together, the bass tunes similarly — and it all fits in quite naturally with everything else that is going on.[1]

The minuet is a real, stately dancing minuet — very different, for instance, from the minuets in the symphonies. The splendidly festive rhythm

goes through the whole piece, and the resolute cadence,

which dominates every eight-bar phrase (this minuet does not allow of any interpolations) underlines the firm character of the dance. In contrast to this, the other dances are not strictly symmetrical (in the contre-danse a four-bar phrase is followed by one of six bars), yet this never upsets the natural flow. Against this brilliant background the action proceeds, mainly in short, half-suppressed exclamations, which are only occasionally extended into longer phrases. Here, too, the characterization is strongly maintained. At the very beginning Donna Elvira, hardly able to contain her feelings, hisses 'Quella è la contadina' with the augmented fourth giving a cutting effect; and when Anna, also agitated, answers with the painful cry, 'io moro!' Ottavio urges them both to keep calm. Then Don Giovanni dances with Zerlina, while Leporello grapples resourcefully with Masetto's ill-tempered stubbornness. Only towards the end, when Don Giovanni drags the now apprehensive Zerlina away, do the three adversaries come close together in expectation of the approaching catastrophe; and this ensues with Zerlina's scream.

---

[1] The tuning of the open strings was a popular joke with the Italians. A later example is the village music in the first scene of Weber's *Freischütz*.

Immediately the whole scene changes with the sudden entry of
E flat major; the dance music breaks off abruptly and the full
orchestra (less horns, trumpets and timpani) realistically depicts
the general confusion in a unison with violent sforzatos. This
Allegro is completely free in form; the harmony also shifts all the
time, from B flat minor via C minor to a half-close full of tension
on the dominant of D minor. Also characteristic are the little
crescendos which precede the entries of the vocal ensemble, while
Zerlina's anxious cries, rising higher and higher, are accompanied
by the violins in syncopation, played piano. Here too all the voices
remain in unison[1], and the two preceding bars for orchestra act
each time as upbeats full of strong suspense. Only at the end,
when Masetto joins the ensemble, do the voices divide again.

But instead of the foreboding D minor tonality we expected,
the key of F major now introduces Don Giovanni and Leporello.
Suitably supported by the orchestra, the two of them act a grand,
pathetic scene for the benefit of the others. Don Giovanni starts,
with the strings presenting a theatrical motif in slurred notes
already familiar from opera seria, energetic dotted rhythms and a
unison trill.[2] Then the comedy continues with imperious string
chords, which Leporello answers below nervous phrases in the
wind. But their opponents are not deceived by this play-acting.
One after another they take off their masks in the most dramatic
fashion, each singing the same phrase in turn (a striking use of
imitative writing); and the strings tell us, with their short tremolo,
that Don Giovanni has completely lost his composure. He can
only stammer odd words, and it is a charming touch that just
here the music sounds very like that of Leporello's fright in the
preceding episode.[3]

Now the characters group themselves differently: on one side
are Zerlina and Masetto, on the other Ottavio with the two ladies,
singing more and more urgently right up to the menacing 'tutto!',
uttered four times. Then, introduced by the familiar tragic unison
theme in the whole orchestra, their indignation finds full expression in a binary movement with a coda, related thematically

---

[1] The same undulating unison figure (though in C major) can be found in the
finale of the second act of Grétry's *Evénements imprévus*.
[2] There is a similar passage in Count Almaviva's aria.
[3] Even the wind accompaniment is the same.

in places to what has gone before. First of all, there is the suspense of the first five bars in F minor, over the pedal note that is reinforced by a timpani roll, the voice of thunder. The crescendo here is suddenly interrupted by both Don Giovanni and Leporello, who is now musically closely united with him. Don Giovanni, incidentally, is not in any way shattered – it is only that his head is reeling at all his misfortunes – and it is a subtle touch that his mind turns not to pathos but to his feast that had started so well. Once again his enemies converge upon him in closed ranks, as the rolling unison of the first Allegro re-appears, now in C major, together with the jagged octave leap; but orchestrally it is all much more tense and increasingly takes on the character of a storm breaking, especially with the triplets that creep in, first in the violins and then eventually spread to all the strings.

Now even Don Giovanni begins to falter. The tension increases noticeably at Donna Anna's long top G on 'trema', below which the middle parts, in thirds, strain upwards in chromatic steps. This provokes more agitation in Don Giovanni and Leporello too, and feverishly their two voices race up the whole C major scale, only to meet irresistible opposition in the form of a harsh dissonance[1] – this passage must not be treated in the buffo manner, but as a violent, desperate assault. Quite logically the indignation of the others now reaches its highest level: their voices climb upwards in powerful unison sequences, ending with the telling phrase:

with the cutting diminished third that has already closed the first part of the ensemble.

This whole section is then repeated, but the climax is kept for the coda; Don Giovanni gathers his courage and succeeds in breaking through his enemies. Once more we catch a breath of his spirit in the forceful theme of the first violins and the glittering descent of the woodwind scale:

---

[1] Note also that the melodic line here goes in the opposite direction.

As the attack on him is renewed with the slurred motif of the opening, he flings at his opponents his Horatian 'se cadesse ancora il mondo, nulla mai temer mi fà' (più stretto), and with a provocative, fanfare-like melody carries the three women with him in immediate musical imitation — surely an intended effect — while the two men, Ottavio and Masetto, form a group by themselves; Leporello naturally rallies to his master.

In this part of the Finale Mozart has no more use for the chorus. That is quite natural. The peasants know better than to interfere in the quarrels of the nobility; when things begin to look risky the musicians and dancers leave the ballroom and let the others pursue their argument amongst themselves. 'Don Giovanni' should not be reduced any more than *Die Zauberflöte* to the status of a grand opera à la Meyerbeer.

Once more Don Giovanni has successfully overcome the dangers with which he is confronted. He knows that none of the women will lay hands on him. Ottavio, as usual, is content with good intentions and verbal threats. As for Masetto, he is too much the country bumpkin and brought up too much in fear of the gentry to take the initiative. The only one with an account to settle is Leporello, who after this latest experience resolves once more to leave his master. But from afar the voice of a stronger power can be discerned in the rolling thunder — a feature pointing to romantic opera. Will the elemental strength in Don Giovanni overcome this too?

As already mentioned, the second act shows a decline in the poetical power of the librettist. Incapable of maintaining the great dramatic sweep with new elements, he is content to extend old ones, and tries to hide this deficiency with all kinds of episodes, mainly in buffo style. These are by no means original, but they are at least skilfully executed and above all have potential for musical treatment. Not until the churchyard scene, which is where he links up again with Bertati, does da Ponte recover his high standard. It is to the credit of the composer that the audience's interest is maintained even through these loose insertions; the reason is that he knew far better than the poet how to keep them connected with the main action.

In this way he powerfully illuminates the inner relationship between master and servant in the little Duet (No. 15). Leporello is utterly dismayed about the part he has had to play in recent events and seriously wishes to give his master notice. Don Giovanni, however, knows how to handle men as well as women. Basically he uses the same procedure with Leporello as with the ladies: he wins him over by deliberately descending to his level of understanding. The only difference is that he establishes the buffo tone from the start and leads the other fellow by the nose from one phrase to the next. The comedy of the piece is that he is merely having fun, whereas the whole thing is deadly earnest for Leporello. Note, for instance, the witty chuckling in the woodwind at Don Giovanni's words, 'che sei matto', countered by Leporello's sullen 'No', his first independent thought, supported by the strings in unison. At the end the same idea re-appears in the orchestra, but without effect, for Leporello has already come to heel, however unwillingly. Even if he still has objections they have to give way to the fulfilment of his heart's desire: to play the master's part himself one day. For Don Giovanni has commanded him to do just this, with Donna Elvira — who now steps on to the balcony. Leporello is to take his place, in order to keep her occupied and clear the way for Don Giovanni to go to her chambermaid.

All this leads to the Terzetto (No. 16) which has always been praised as a pearl of Mozartian ensemble writing. Clearly laid out in ternary form (with a varied da capo of the first section), it is also thematically homogeneous, for apart from the more adventurous middle section it consists of a few basic ideas that keep recurring. And once more drama and music are united in a wonderful way.

It is not only the thoughts and feelings of the people concerned that speak to us through their music, but also their whole environment. After only eight bars we sense what it is that made Elvira come out on the balcony: the harmony between her mood and the southern summer night. Here again we are confronted with one of those quite modern descriptions of nature which reveal the mysterious movement of natural forces in musical terms, without any rococo colouring.[1] The enigmatic air that pervades this piece is

---

[1] Cf. the aria Susanna sings in the garden.

Don Giovanni's strongest ally. Everything works towards the same goal: the key of A major, the smooth orchestration (without oboes, for the first time in the opera), and the gently floating principal tune. Now that Elvira believes herself to be alone and undisturbed by the stresses of the outside world, she gives voice to her most intimate emotion: her love for Don Giovanni which, as an immediate witness of his unfaithfulness, she has so far only been able to show in the form of hatred. Longingly she gazes into the night and enters into a discourse with her heart which still beats with warm affection for him despite his infidelity. But even here she remains the true Elvira: at the thought of the 'empio traditore' the violins suddenly dart upwards in impassioned scale passages, such as we have already met in her first aria, and the struggle within her heart is expressed most movingly at the words 'è colpa aver pietà'.

Now Leporello sings the second principal theme of the piece:[1]

zit - to di Donn' El - vi - ra

whose slinking secretive character is an apt expression of the plot they have laid under cover of night. Don Giovanni then intervenes on behalf of his puppet, Leporello. As always, he begins with the same melody as Elvira but enhanced by its new key of E major, and by the addition of a sensuous glow. Now that strange second theme also takes a hold on Elvira ('Numi! che strano affetto'); it is masterly how Mozart, on the basis of these two contrasting moods, tightens the threads of the conspiracy more and more. Next we have a short, typically Mozartian transition, with a surprising modulation and chromatic melody together with a short crescendo to a sùbito piano, which suddenly lead to C major. Now Don Giovanni no longer sings in Elvira's way but in his own. It is perhaps the most seductive tune we ever hear from him, and it is surely not by accident that the beginning is exactly the same as the following Canzonetta.[2] Still, it should not be assumed

---

[1] The step of a fourth at the end is missing in the instrumental parts. Later, when they do have it, it can be seen that its second note is really meant as an upbeat of the subsequent repetition.

[2] In the second phrase it also has its suspension on the fourth, with an accentuated passing note on the fifth; cf. Zerlina's aria (No. 13).

that Don Giovanni is already thinking of Elvira's chambermaid. It is much more likely that under the spell of the setting, his fiery sensuality expresses itself without any particular object, and that the alluring melody is addressed not to one woman but to womankind in general. When, immediately afterwards, he returns to this mood with mandolin chords and dance rhythms for the benefit of the little servant girl, it amounts to a diminution of the same feeling, that sounds like irony against himself.

As so often with Mozart, this fiery outburst is followed by an equally strong response — Elvira's last gesture of resistance, in a passionate, sharply accentuated melody over a tremolo in the strings. With the syncopation in the violins at her last 'non ti credo' (another crescendo followed by sùbito piano) the struggle reaches it climax. Here the cynic in Don Giovanni comes to the fore in his pathetic 'O m'uccido!', calling forth Leporello's delicious and truly Italian, 'io rido'. While he chuckles away happily, however, Elvira is finally defeated. Once again, the purely musical development, modulating back from C to A major, coincides with that of the drama — with Elvira's change of attitude; and with the return to the original key, all three unite in the principal theme. Beautifully effective here is the way in which Elvira sings with Leporello, who in this cruel situation feels something like pity for the victim, while Don Giovanni complacently congratulates himself on his victory. Naturally, though, the sinister second theme also returns, gradually dominating both voices and orchestra. In addition, a big crescendo gets under way and the development seems to converge towards a climax of excitement, when it sinks once again to a piano. A staccato motif of only two notes in the orchestra depicts with inspired subtlety the fluctuations that have occurred during the whole episode.

Typical Mozart! He has not the slightest interest in crude dramatic explosions, and feels with unerring instinct that the romantic suspense of the situation, which so peculiarly blends feminine devotion and ruthless masculine egoism in its most seductive form, would not gain in the least by such treatment. At the same time he underplays the crudity of the action, and the buffoonery suggested by the librettist, not in order to conceal it but simply because he sees more behind it than da Ponte, who, like all ordinary men, considered what he could see at a glance was more real, and what promised the greatest effect more vital. For an Italian the masquerade would have been the main concern; for Mozart it is the interplay of internal, spiritual forces, their mutual attraction and repulsion, in the framework of the mysterious workings of nature. Where in this picture would there have been room for anything shallow, coarse or 'effective'?

The connexion between the Terzetto and the Canzonetta (No. 17) has already been mentioned. Again we are watching a scene from everyday life; such serenades were quite common on mild summer nights in Vienna. The accompanying mandolin was most probably familiar to Mozart for the same reason. He had already written songs with mandolin accompaniment; in opera the use of the instrument was known to him from the works of Paisiello[1] and Grétry. The folk-like character, however, shows itself not only in the instrumentation, but also in the simple strophic form of the song[2] and the strictly symmetrical division into phrases.[3] All this is intended for the chambermaid. Nevertheless, it is not a naive little street song. Whether one assumes that Don Giovanni is singing a well-known tune or that he is improvising the serenade himself, it is by no means removed from his own world of feeling. Only he of all men could sing a song of such intoxicating sensuous warmth. Its similarity to the Terzetto merely proves that Don Giovanni is still in the same mood: it only acquires a shade of irony from its popular vein and its exaggerated words like 'pianto', 'morire' etc. The singer certainly feels what he sings, but he is also consciously enjoying his superiority, which in this case promises him an easy victory; playing these high-spirited games is also part of his nature.

---

[1] In his 'Barbiere'; also in the Canzonetta in Traetta's *Festo d'Imeneo*. It is worth remarking, all the same, that Mozart completely avoids the chirping note repetitions, so popular with the others.

[2] In the Introduction to Anfossi's *Geloso in cimento*, the serenade begins like this:

ca - ra vi ven - go a dir   ch'a - mor mi fa   lan - guir   ch'a - mor mi fa   lan - guir

[3] Only the interludes are in two-bar phrases, again following popular usage. The scheme of modulation also adheres strictly to the simple Lied character. The first part modulates to the dominant, the second returns via the relative minor of the subdominant and the subdominant itself to the tonic, as in countless Italian serenades.

Meanwhile his plans are thwarted again. Masetto arrives with his peasant friends, to take revenge in his own way on the man who has disturbed his happiness. The style of the text is now entirely that of opera buffa: Leporello disguised as Don Giovanni, the peasants waiting for a fight — these are well-worn ideas from the oldest examples of the species. With such adversaries Don Giovanni naturally has no difficulty in mastering the situation. As Leporello, he simply takes command of the whole affair, and the aria (No. 18) that he sings in the role of his servant is one of the most ingenious notions in the whole opera.

The text contents itself with a simple account of the situation: sentries are posted, the enemies are described with precision — musically a fairly meagre proposition. Mozart naturally also makes use of the buffo idiom here and depicts all the actual events scrupulously. But at the same time he fills this framework with an abundant inner life. For Don Giovanni, while feeling quite at ease in Leporello's mask, also likes to play his own superior game with it, lifting it every now and then, but in such a way that the stupid fellows are unaware of it; he positively wallows in his ironic self-characterization, and provokes their dull-wittedness again and again. Above all, his violent demoniacal nature keeps breaking through in his unbounded delight at providing these bumpkins, who have the audacity to assault him, with the lesson they deserve. Thus the aria is a typically Mozartian creation, cohesive and yet with an almost inexhaustible variety of sensations.

Its external form corresponds with this. Basically it is in three sections; but it also has features of rondo form, for the da capo contains new ideas, while the epilogue reverts again to the main theme. This begins softly, but full of tension, with a long held note on the horns and syncopating violins in an energetic, authoritative vein, supported by imperious gestures in the rest of the orchestra. But as early as the eleventh bar the picture changes: with delightful bassoon passages in thirds and short trills in the oboes and violins Don Giovanni describes, at first still in Leporello's manner, what usually happens in his amorous escapades. Meanwhile his own face already seems to shine through the mask in the ominous syncopated passage at 'ferite pur'.[1] Then,

---

[1] Already in Scene V of Philidor's *Blaise* (1759), there are similar syncopations in the orchestra at Blaisène's words 'il me bat le scélérat'.

in C major, comes Don Giovanni's ironic description of himself in which, as throughout the aria, the lion's share falls to the orchestra. There he actually stands before us, complete with flowing plumes in his hat. But once again, something incites him well and truly to play the devil. The passage:

with its diabolical trill goes far beyond the realm of Leporello, and he continues his dual role in what follows. After the return of the opening, he sends the peasants packing quite brutally so that he can deal with Masetto alone — and here there is a shift to the subdominant typical of Mozart. With Masetto he shows even less retraint. First of all he firmly keeps him back, plainly to make a fool of him, in the characteristic passage:[1]

in double octaves in the strings (though only in two-part harmony) and with its cheeky echo in the woodwind. He becomes more and more contemptuous: the motif C - A, incessantly repeated, seems positively infamous, particularly as it is taken up by the orchestra in various guises. The piece ends with a long coda, based on the theme with which Don Giovanni had originally chased away the peasants. He and Masetto walk up and down a little in the side streets, and the music of the aria follows them, half mockingly, gradually ebbing away. Thus this curious piece whose element of disguise again demands a considerable gift of mimicry, fades away like a shadow in the dark.

But the storm that has been gathering over Masetto's unsuspecting head now breaks; Don Giovanni slashes at him with the back of his sword, a punishment quite appropriate for someone like him in opera buffa. At this moment Zerlina appears and comforts him in her aria (No. 19). She is neither horrified nor sentimental, but she appreciates the absurdity of the bridegroom's plight and probably considers the punishment a fitting one for his

---

[1] Mozart notates the second bar incorrectly and writes, as usual, A flat instead of G sharp.

jealousy. But true love never dies and the medicine she offers to cure him is entirely in accordance with her nature. The text also expresses this, with the directness that was usual in opera buffa; Mozart, however, does not labour the obvious here any more than he does in the duet between Papageno and Papagena. True, there is an underlying sensuality, in which the softer colours of the orchestra play a part (flutes, clarinets and horns; no oboes!). The melody too, with its affectionate, feminine suspensions[1] sounds like a foretaste of love's bliss. Yet over everything there is a veil of charming grace, which does not allow the human element to predominate and turns nature into art; here, again, is the hand of genius. Anything glaring is avoided; the music hardly stirs from the original key.

The aria consists of two parts. The first, which remains in a popular vein[2] both in expression and in the way in which the themes follow one another, presents the basic feeling behind the whole; it contains a multitude of endearing phrases, like that in the cellos in the third and fourth bars, the numerous little trills and, above all, the enchanting wind writing. The second part, which follows after a pause on which she gives him a long and loving look, uses again in both text and music the imagery of the beating heart, employed in many varied ways since the time of Pergolesi. But here, too, Mozart is not concerned with music as a method of painting. He intentionally emphasizes Zerlina's urgency, as is illustrated by the unison figure in the three wind instruments over the quivering pedal note; indeed this second part is generally designed as an intensification of the first. The instruments take the lead; the gently descending octave passage in the violins against the staccato tapping in the wind is particularly ingenious. But in the voice there is also an increase of emotional intensity in the little motif that strains upwards towards the seventh; at the last 'sentilo battere, toccami quà' it can hardly control its longing, and with the repeated 'quà' the caressing trills from the first part

---

[1] There is already an unusual warmth in the seventh and eighth bars, with the unexpected wind entry.

[2] The warmth is German in style; this type of melody with its rhythm $\frac{3}{8}\,\sqcap\!\sqcap\,|\,\sqcap\!\sqcap$ is however, Italian throughout and very frequent in similar pieces by Majo and Piccinni, for instance.

appear again. But Mozart goes no further in this sensuous vein: one more playful rocking figure in the woodwind, and grace keeps the upper hand. The piece ends with a marvellously warm outburst in the full orchestra, combining the themes of both parts; as so often with Mozart, it dies away pianissimo.

The Sextet (No. 20) marks the end of the buffo part of the second act. With the nocturnal confusions and the mounting imbroglio caused by the appearance of more and more characters just at the critical moment and by the threats to poor Leporello, it has all the ingredients of a genuine piece of opera buffa. This is also true of da Ponte's treatment, which in the second part even dismisses the effect of the imbroglio on everyone concerned with a few quite ordinary, well-worn phrases. For the Italians this would have been the opportunity for a sparkling and musically effective conclusion to the whole entanglement. But for Mozart it was quite another matter.

His writing for this scene has always inspired the greatest admiration; indeed it is one of the most brilliant examples of his own peculiar skill in blending tragedy and comedy. The sublime and the ridiculous, the profoundest and most trivial notions are constantly presented side by side. But dramatically, as well, this is far more than a buffo piece. What for da Ponte was just a scene to fill up his second act, became for Mozart an organic link in a vast dramatic structure. For despite his absence, the actual hero of the Sextet is not Leporello but Don Giovanni. This is not only because he is represented by his servant — though in Leporello's present state of dejection over the collapse of the whole masquerade it is more his own character that emerges than his master's — but also because the others are clearly under Don Giovanni's spell. His adversaries suspect that he is involved once again in this latest comedy, and for the last time before his downfall they all unite in their common hatred of him, though with a sense of impotence in face of his daemonic power. Without knowing it, it is to be the last victory that he wins over his enemies, before his insatiable desire drives him into the arms of a power superior even to his. But the music with which they express their sorrow in the second part of the Sextet touches on the profoundest human sentiments and rises above even the highest theatrical

105

level to the most radiant summit of art. Indeed there could have
been no better foil for the powerful second Finale than this
ensemble, which raises Don Giovanni's enemies to the heights of
true humanity.

Meanwhile Leporello stands there, naked and exposed, a
wretched creature prepared to sacrifice everything to save his life,
even the outward guise and inner essence of the master of whom
he was once so proud. The old theatrical role of the jester, whose
main function has always been to mediate between actors and
audience, could not have been fitted more ingeniously into the
drama. One subtle feature is the way in which, after Leporello is
unmasked, the others become indifferent towards him; they have
nothing more to do with the poor fellow.[1]

The musical ground-plan is of the greatest uniformity, consisting as it does of two large sections, an Andante and an Allegro
molto in the same key of E flat major. All the more free is the
inner structure, especially of the Andante; but cohesion is restored not only by the repetition of certain passages, but also by
the return of some of the same orchestral themes, so that something like a free rondo form emerges. After an introduction of
only two bars, such as Mozart loved to use to add a touch of
suspense, Elvira begins, alarmed at the darkness of the place to
which her supposed lover has led her. That she is highly emotional is made plain by the sforzato leap of a seventh in bar 4, by
the impassioned violin figure in bar 7 (already familiar from her
earlier music) and above all by the end of the phrase in bar 11
with its strange chromatic unison in the orchestra. It is, however,
the touching quality of the beginning that immediately engages
our sympathy.[2]

The contrast in Leporello's part is all the sharper. Groping and
fumbling, his only thought is how to get out of this dire situation.
At first he is pretty faint-hearted, but when at last he finds 'that
wretched door' the orchestra trills contentedly, and with one of
Mozart's most telling orchestral unisons he decides to escape; one

---

[1] Schaul, in *Letters on Musical Taste*, mentions the Sextet as an instance of
Mozart's offending against common sense, as it was written in tragic style
when it ought to be in demi-caractère.
[2] The opening calls to mind Leonora's great aria in the first act of *Fidelio*
('Komm, Hoffnung, lass den letzten Stern').

can positively see him tip-toeing in great agitation towards the door. But unfortunately it is the wrong one; with a modulation as swift as it is unexpected (involving an enharmonic change in which B flat major becomes the lowered submediant of D major), Donna Anna and Ottavio enter with torch-bearers and bar his way.

With its bright trumpet sounds, this new key of D major has an almost physically forceful effect; something like a shaft of light suddenly falls across the scene, not only preventing Leporello's escape but also banishing the dark powers of deception and trickery[1]. With the sincerity that is so characteristic of him, Ottavio consoles his beloved; it is the same warm and noble type of cantilena with which he comforted her at the beginning of the first act. While the first violins in the buffo manner maintain the same motif — one very common in Mozart — the semiquaver figure in the second violins reflects Ottavio's deep inner turmoil. But Donna Anna's grief will find peace only in the grave. It is a subtle feature that at first she tries to enter into the tone of her lover — her reply has the same orchestral accompaniment — but this tone immediately changes in quality as she sings. Not only does the key of D minor typify this, but above all the melodic line of her opening phrase:

which has already twice been heard as the symbol of her wounded heart. Both times it was in D minor: in her first duet and then in the Finale of the first act, a further proof of the consistent way in which Mozart delineates character. The radiance of D major is soon extinguished: Donna Anna's melody, corresponding to her character, drifts more and more into emotional pathos (note the eloquent repeated grace-note on 'sol') and ends with a melancholy chromatic lament in C minor.

Now begins the strangest episode of the whole section, the realism of which contains something positively frightening — for comedy here is also tragic and tragedy borders on the grotesque. Elvira and Leporello return to the foreground with the following orchestral figure, which from now on appears again and again during the Andante:

---

[1] Compare this with the last movement of the C minor Serenade. There is also a similar passage in *La Finta Giardiniera*.

with its twitching rhythm and its melody winding chromatically downwards[1], it is strangely equivocal and oscillates between tragedy and comedy. In immediate succession it accompanies Elvira, whose fate turns towards tragedy at this moment, as she again fears that she is losing her supposed lover when she has only just won him back, and Leporello, who in great agitation again tries to slip away. He eventually returns to his earlier unison motif, though much more dejectedly, in the minor.

One can feel that the drama is building up to a climax, and it comes with the entry of Zerlina and Masetto, followed immediately by the unmasking of Leporello. At once the music takes on a more pathetic mode of expression.[2] All except Elvira unite in calling for vengeance on the traitor, while, to everyone's astonishment, Elvira intercedes for her beloved: 'è mio marito! pietà!' She sings these words in the utmost anxiety, accompanied by a chromatic theme whose melancholy apsect is further reinforced by the sustained line in the violas. This exclamation marks her most tragic moment; those few notes contain the very essence of her being, her fervent devotion to Don Giovanni. The others inevitably respond to her mood. Their homophony relaxes into more diffuse, at first imitative, part writing, in which the individuals are sharply differentiated; the orchestra, on the other hand, holds on steadily to the chromatic theme. Only at the sudden forte entry of the full orchestra do the voices reunite, proclaiming in unison 'morrà!', with a vicious leap of a seventh.

In mounting desperation Elvira once more repeats her plea for mercy, but in vain. Then as Leporello raises his voice, the music moves at last into the key of G minor, prepared long before but delayed again and again by interrupted cadences. And now he too is in such desperate straits that, like Elvira, his inmost nature is revealed. The skills he learned from Don Giovanni are not equal to this assault. He abandons both his master's outward aspect and the playing of his part, and stands before the others as a miserable rogue, whining for his life to be spared.

This becomes positively grotesque, his 'quasi piangendo'

---

[1] Moreover it is consistently doubled at the octave, and only appears in the strings.

[2] The violin motif in the second bar is related to Elvira's other themes (see the beginning of the Sextet, bar 7).

sounding more like a howl than a song. He gets stuck on certain phrases and repeats them over and over again, stopping completely for a while on long, drawn-out notes. And yet everything is expressed with scrupulous detail: first his wretched whining for mercy with its chromatic avoidance of the tonic, then his desperate confession 'quello io non sono', turning to the dominant, and finally his 'viver lasciatemi per carità', which rises frantically in the subdominant key (note the crescendo!) and then, on the sharp dissonance of a ninth, collapses in a downward seventh to which he utters his final, pathetic whimper. Here, as if paralyzed, the cellos and basses remain rooted on their long notes, while the violins double the voice in octaves[1] and that same weeping chromatic figure ripples downwards five times running, in double octaves in the wind — a most creepy effect.[2] At his last 'per carità' Leporello loses the support of the orchestra; only the oboes, who have so far been silent, join in his last plea. All this is pervaded by the key of G minor, Mozart's tonality of anguish, which here also appears in an ironic light.

Once again this Leporello episode is answered by the rest of the ensemble, except that they now enter together from the start. The sotto voce in which they all express their surprise is truly Mozartian: only the unexpected jolt into the new key and the change of orchestral colour reveal the volte-face in the situation. This sotto voce rings much more true and is more natural than any theatrical storm of indignation, delivered forte. Only two bars later does anger at the deception break through with sharp rhythmic definition. The contrasting pair of phrases is repeated a tone higher, and the marked emphasis on the word 'Leporello' should be especially noticed. At the end of the Andante, however, the familiar chromatic theme returns again, portraying the tense and fluctuating situation most poetically. After all, everyone in the group fears yet another infamous stratagem on Don Giovanni's part, and the Andante ends with their anxious question ('che mai sarà') on the dominant of C minor.

The monumental Molto Allegro section answers it for them, though not in a way that lightens the strain on their emotions. Leporello, who created the whole situation, becomes less and less

---

[1] The ornamentation in the second phrase has a powerful effect.
[2] The little crescendo here should not be overlooked.

important, while their sense of disillusionment and impotence in face of this new and uncanny example of Don Giovanni's scheming breaks through all the more strongly. It manifests itself in utter amazement, impassioned grief and resigned sorrow one after the other. And it is precisely these that were of particular importance to Mozart, as is clear from the sustained writing for the voices and especially the wonderful polyphonic passage in the coda. Here grief is transformed into the most profound melancholy, inspired by the general tragedy of man's fate. There are passages, moreover, where Mozart preferred a deeply intimate tone (sotto voce and piano) to the volume of sound the text might seem to suggest. In other words, instead of becoming the uproarious ending that the Italians would have expected, this section is the true climax of the whole Sextet.

Even so, Mozart does not lose sight of the humorous side of the situation: he even emphasizes it by letting Leporello be the first to take the lead. The latter begins to sense that the wind has turned in his favour, and despite his fears for his life he summons up fresh courage. The accompaniment, in which the flute doubles the vocal line — as it often does for Don Giovanni — shows clearly that his old self is gradually coming to the surface. Indeed, he even succeeds in carrying the others along with him thematically — for they echo his phrase in diminution[1] — since they too are completely stupified. But their outburst destroys his composure once more: he starts chattering hurriedly and races in a crescendo up to his top B flat, again accompanied in unison. Now the ensemble takes on a darker colour. Despair at being exposed again to Don Giovanni's stratagems strikes them with full force ('Che giornata' etc.) And again we notice the effect on Leporello, who naturally has no conception of the way their minds work, but hears in every sound a threat to himself. He, too, senses something uncanny, but only in his own grotesque way; this is evident from his parlando on the two notes A and B flat, and from the figure alternating rapidly between strings and wind that seems to weigh so heavily on him.

Then follows the first of those sotto voce passages with descending violin scales, a strange mixture of grief and oppression.

---

[1] This diminution also affects the metrical structure: five bars of Leporello correspond to three of the others.

Leporello now retires more into the background, though naturally retaining his independence and reacting in his own fashion to the new turn in the situation. As if transfixed, the others stay rooted in ponderous dotted rhythms to the chord of E flat major, until it gives way quite abruptly (musically, too, an 'impensata novità') to the chord of D flat major — a sudden outburst of fear, shattering in its impact. Even Leporello is shaken: as if quaking with terror, he exclaims on his high D flat just after the others. Here the ensemble splits up into completely separate groups, within which the individual characters stand out clearly. Thus Donna Anna's numbness soon melts into an extensive coloratura, sinking to a piano with the most affecting expression of sorrow. Then excitement flares up again with the repeated 'mille torbidi pensieri'; this time it is Elvira whose passionate temperament goes its own confused way. Then this whole section is repeated from Leporello's first parlando, and is followed, after a portentous interrupted cadence, by the vast coda, during which Leporello's character disappears completely in the ensemble as a whole. Here the music, by delaying the actual conclusion with numerous interpolations, raises grief to a mystical level. This process begins at the point where the upper parts between them hold on to their high F while the cellos and basses circle round B flat; and there is an expression even of religious feeling in the expanded cadence, with its strict ecclesiastical polyphony. The following episode with its disjointed crotchets and the strong emphasis on 'novità' adds further to the impression of mystery; and immediately afterwards the Sextet reaches its musical climax in a passage of inspired a cappella writing. Here the opera buffa lies far behind us, and it is significant that Leporello does not sing in this passage. Only in the final bars does he again play a prominent role and thus this inspired piece returns at the end to the situation from which it started.

In his Sextet Mozart transformed a piece of opera buffa convention into a portrayal of living characters that is far superior to anything called tragic or comic in the opera of his time, touching as it does on the fundamentals of human existence. Once more the construction is both dramatically and musically perfect. The Allegro is a movement in two sections with a kind of introduction

111

and a coda. Its emotional content is so varied that not only do the repeats not weaken the general effect, but they are even felt to be dramatically necessary. The grouping (Leporello against the others) is carried through with admirable symmetry, evident not only in the orchestration but also in the harmonic structure. The ensemble never leaves the home key of E flat major,[1] while Leporello is always straining towards the dominant, though without being able to settle there. The piece is altogether a striking indication of how little harmonic display Mozart needs to achieve his purpose. Melody, rhythm, part-writing, orchestration and, last but not least, dynamics, play a much greater part. That he did not make a hard and fast rule about harmonic economy is shown by the Andante of the Sextet with its much wider range of modulations. But there he is concerned with the continuing action, while the basic character of the Allegro is one of lyrical description, keeping the same fundamental mood in varying shades. Temporary deviations on individual words like 'novità' do not cancel out the effect of the home key; in fact they strengthen it.

Leporello's aria (No. 21) brings the situation created by the Sextet to a conclusion, so far as he himself is concerned. The pressure on him has been relaxed, and soon enough the sly old fox comes before us again. At the beginning his head still seems to be swimming, for the first few bars are distinctly reminiscent of a theme in the Sextet. It is a genuine buffo aria addressed to everyone in turn and demanding a good deal of 'action'. The form is binary with a free arrangement of the thematic material in which the crafty little motif in bars 8ff is most important and finally even helps him to escape. There are delightful episodes, such as 'il padron con prepotenza l'innocenza mi rubò', with its imperious start and almost pious continuation. The music is also consistently suited to the character of each person to whom he turns. Only towards the end, when he reaches Ottavio, does it assume a mysterious quality, beginning with a grotesque canon between strings and wind. One can almost see him, gradually groping his way towards the door and finally slinking through it.

Now Ottavio too realizes that Don Giovanni, his peer, has slain the Commendatore; and he resolves to seek the vengeance for which he is uniquely qualified as a man and as an aristocrat. But the

---

[1] The modulation to D flat is only transient.

fact that he wants to hand him over to the law strikes us as cold,
if not absurd. Don Giovanni has assailed the honour of his bride;
and besides this, he has not merely stabbed the Commendatore in
the back but killed him in open duel. The proper way for a nobleman to punish him is not by civil law, but in the same way that
he has been attacked, by the sword. Of course, Ottavio knows
quite well that it is no less dangerous to haul Don Giovanni before
a judge, as the text of his aria tells us; so it is not that he is lacking
in courage. Still, it would all have been far more plausible if da
Ponte had given up the idea of the law.

All in all, Don Ottavio has given scholars a great deal of trouble.[1]
Da Ponte makes him a colourless youth. In the first act, however,
the faults in his characterization are not too glaring; it is true that
his behaviour is always passive, but it is noble and distinguished
throughout, and his sincere affection for Donna Anna wins our
sympathy. That he does not draw his sword in the first Finale is
not so absurd, for at that stage he is not yet convinced of Don
Giovanni's guilt and has really no reason to challenge him to a
duel for his assault on a village wench.[2] In the second act, on the
other hand, it is he who pays the price for the halting dramatic
movement already discussed. He fades more and more into the
background, and it seems altogether too late when he finally
decides to act.

It is impossible to believe that Mozart was not aware of the
weakness of Don Ottavio's character. Like da Ponte, he also
treats him as a secondary figure, though in his own way. With
Ottavio, love is the fundamental motive for all action, as it is with
Don Giovanni; but while it unleashes all the latter's energy, it
thoroughly paralyses Ottavio's. Apart from his love for Donna
Anna, there is scarcely another thought in his mind, and the

---

[1] Chrysander presumes that Mozart influenced Ottavio's characterization in
the same way as he did that of Donna Anna, which is certainly probable. But
when he suggests that da Ponte turned Bertati's character into a weakling he
definitely goes too far: for in Bertati's libretto Ottavio behaves just as
passively, only his portrait is far more sketchy. Among more recent writers,
M. Kalbeck has tried to present him as a character of more importance while
Schurig sees him as a tragi-comic figure.
[2] The idea of his confronting Don Giovanni with a pistol without firing it is
also unfortunate, since it makes him more 'active' but quite unnecessarily
throws doubt on his courage.

thunderclaps of fate resounding all around him reach his ear as if from the faint distance. This explains his lack of initiative. Whenever he is compelled to act, it is reason, not will-power that drives him to it. The result is a fire of straw, quickly dying out because the innermost part of his personality is not involved. As always with such characters, sincerely meant words have to take the place of action. In this figure, standing between characters like Don Giovanni and Donna Anna, there is doubtless a conscious irony on the author's part that would have tempted many a composer to caricature him, however gently. But here again Mozart does not sit in judgement on his own creations. He lets Ottavio make the effect his particular character and his relationship to his environment would produce. He even gives him the noblest and most warmly inspired melodies in the whole opera; one need only compare them with Don Giovanni's to understand how different they are in their attitude to love. Ottavio never becomes sentimental in a distasteful, effeminate way: what he feels is true, sincere affection, and his weakness consists only in the fact that after taking the first oath his love absorbs him so completely that all energetic impulses simply waste away. Apart from this, he also attaches great importance to outward appearances in the behaviour of a nobleman. So he is a convincing character, isolated in a world of wild passions. He is certainly not an embarrassing figure in the drama, as so many inept performers like to present him, but an organic part of the action, indissolubly bound up with Donna Anna's fate as well as with that of Don Giovanni.

Ottavio's aria (No. 22) reflects his nature with particular truthfulness. The situation forces him to act, and he is fully aware of the bitter contest that lies ahead. Yet love is foremost in his thoughts, and it is this that he expresses in the first part of this binary composition with quite exquisite warmth and sweetness, and without any pathos (the music is marked Andante grazioso). Here the noble lyricism that typifies his entire role reaches its highest level. Certain virtuoso features, such as the long sustained F^1 and the various florid passages, were obviously included for the benefit of the tenor Baglioni. All the same, they are not there just for their

---

[1] Rubini, instead of holding the F for its full length, used to sing an A with the violins on their trill. Whether the additional virtuosity is really in Mozart's style is a matter of opinion.

own sake, and at the recapitulation it is the coloratura that achieves with particular subtlety the transition from the heroic mood of the second part back to the first theme. But this show of strength is also in keeping with Ottavio's nature: the orchestra, it is true, displays much energy, but the voice remains curiously irresolute and conveys this new sentiment with far less conviction than the preceding one. This has sometimes been considered a deficiency in the aria, but in fact it fits in excellently with the picture of the man's character. The situation is the same when the passage returns in the second half, where the expression is in some respects more intense: the coloratura with its wide intervals even touches on the convulsive, theatrical style of the Neapolitans. It is all the more convincing when the orchestral epilogue returns to the gentle mood.

In the churchyard scene da Ponte turns again to Bertati, whom he occasionally copies even to the extent of using the same words; Don Giovanni's destiny is at a decisive turning point, but this time not through a clash with mortal opponents, in which he could always show himself superior. Amorous adventures give way to a new element: the outrage against the dead.[1] Nevertheless, this will seem a break with the past only to those who think of Don Giovanni as being solely concerned with his love affairs. His field is in fact much wider: in anything to do with the sensual forces he feels himself to be master. For the same reason the dead simply do not exist for him, for they are removed from the world of the senses. He neither fears nor respects them, and for him a churchyard is a place like any other in which to make light and witty conversation.

Da Ponte has aptly inserted a new diversion, the attempt on Leporello's lady love; and it is at this moment that the statue of the Commendatore suddenly begins to speak. The music points directly to the Oracle in Gluck's *Alceste,* and beyond that to Rameau — witness the declamation on one note, the unusual orchestration and the singular pathos. But here, too, Mozart remains himself, as is shown not only by the changes of time signature and key, but above all by the inspired touch of melan-

---

[1] As a model for the scenery Schnerich rightly suggests the Salic graves in Verona.

choly which colours the words of the statue, though he is made of stone; one need only follow the chromatic line of the first bassoon in the second Adagio. And the sequence of harmonies is consistent with this: the ghost begins in the tragic key of D minor and finishes in G minor![1]

A power that is removed from his own sensual world has entered Don Giovanni's life; a daemonic being like himself, but free from the limitations of human existence and therefore superior to him from the outset. That the ghost does not intervene on behalf of any moral law in the ordinary sense has already been said often enough, and it would have been a mistake to weaken the dramatic movement of the work by moralizing just before its powerful final climax. There is certainly a moral element in Don Giovanni's downfall, but in the wider sense of the evaluation of reality. The point of the opera is not to proclaim a universal moral, but to depict the decisive battle between two tremendous forces. We sense the ultimate connexion between even the most restless, passion-ridden human existence and the whole universe.

The words of the statue at once arouse superstitious fears in Leporello. Don Giovanni, however, takes it all as a jest made by someone quite outside his own world and tries to humour him with his invitation. Thus even the final catastrophe is introduced in the buffo manner, and the irony is further emphasized by the fact that it is Leporello, trembling with fear, who delivers the invitation to the Statue. This creates the occasion for the curious duet (No. 24), in which the key of E major is striking in its sultriness. In romantic opera the dark *genius loci* and the fearful aspect of the situation would probably have been the main points of interest. But it is precisely here that Mozart is so restrained, letting it appear only on the periphery. The statue has already revealed his supernatural being in the preceding recitative, and in the Finale is to dominate the scene completely. So in this duet only Don Giovanni and Leporello are to occupy the foreground.

The beginning even seems to accord with Don Giovanni's idea that it is all an entertaining illusion. Leporello forces himself to adopt once again the major-domo tone that he had used to invite

---

[1] Mörike's splendid poetic description of this passage is as follows: 'As if from remote starry spheres, the sound of silver trombones, ice-cold, cutting through body and soul, descends through the blue night.'

the three masked guests in the first act. However, his collapse as early as the fourth bar is suspicious, and at the following phrase with its leap of a seventh:[1]

Pad - ron,   mi tre-ma il   co - re, non   pos - so, non pos-so ter-mi - nar!

his composure completely vanishes. Don Giovanni upbraids him impatiently, though his anxiety obviously adds to his amusement. So Leporello begins his speech again, this time in the higher key of B major, but much more timidly as his terror increases. At that moment he sees his master's flashing sword, and in mortal fear (again in unison with the strings) he gathers the remainder of his strength for a third attempt delivered in a tense and grotesque fashion.[2] The cellos and basses are silent; against a tapping pedal note in the violas on the dominant of B major, a short whispering motif appears in the violins and is echoed in the woodwind, accompanied by effective syncopated writing. Later both violins and wind are divided and as a result there are suspensions of quite extraordinary severity.

Leporello himself, however, has lost all sense of dignity; he stammers out his speech on two notes, and when he finally thinks he sees the statue nod he is frozen with horror. At his interrupted cadence on G the music suddenly rises above the buffo sphere to a more serious idiom, foreshadowing the style of the Finale. Urged on by Don Giovanni, Leporello at last tells him what he has seen ('colla marmorea testa' etc.), faithfully imitating the nod in a state of extreme terror. Don Giovanni parodies him with cutting irony, but then his old instinct begin to stir: he must get to the bottom of

---

[1] This interval also plays a prominent part in the Sextet.

[2] Compare this with Pasquariello's typically Italian invitation in Gazzaniga's score:

the affair. His own address to the Statue, introduced by an uncanny interrupted cadence going to C major, removes him, too, from the realm of the opera buffa[1] ; he becomes much more forceful, already fore-shadowing his heroic behaviour when he is confronted with the ghost later on.

In fact this unexpected modulation changes the atmosphere completely. The sparkling buffo idiom seems to have disappeared;[2] accompanied only by two horns, the statue answers Don Giovanni's question, which had been asked emphatically on the dominant, with its 'si' on the tonic. This is all that Mozart found necessary to represent such an unheard-of scene: the statue is to make its effect more than anything else through its *voice*. But the horn call drags on into the next section, like a fatal omen, summoning the other wind instruments to join it. The unexpected use of the chromatically lowered submediant, C natural, very different in its effect here from its appearance eleven bars earlier, intensifies the sinister impact of the scene, especially by leaving the harmony to the imagination. Even Don Giovanni can hardly free himself from his little phrase which turns erratically this way and that.

But now the buffo element creeps in again, shedding a curiously ambiguous light on the piece from now on. While Don Giovanni's thoughts are already directed towards the pleasures of the table, and Leporello longs only to get away from this gruesome place, a strange excitement starts up in the orchestra and the atmosphere, veering between horror and frantic gaiety, reaches a climax of intensity and then dies away as the two men disappear in the darkness.[3] One need only compare Mozart's approach with Gazzaniga's, in whose work the horror of the place serves only as a piquant but illusory stage effect, to realize his genius to the full. And it is the same when one thinks of later composers in similar

---

[1] In Gazzaniga's opera there is a slow Siciliano in D minor at this point which with its solo passages for wind instruments has a most picturesque character.
[2] Gazzaniga's version also has ponderous dotted rhythms here, although he weakens their impact by adding, after Don Giovanni's question in the Phrygian mode, a second question on dominant and tonic.
[3] A colourful feature is the augmentation of the last motif in the violas, beginning in the third bar from the end. The semiquaver movement at this point is also found in Gazzaniga, but as a simple tremolo. He does not have the gruesome passage, 'mover mi posso appena'.

scenes, where the romanticism of nature is treated as the main point of interest. With Mozart, the psychological element is always in the foreground; the supernatural enters only when it is necessary to create that curious tingling excitement which increases the suspense before the approaching catastrophe, without anticipating its overpowering effect.

The duet is also remarkable in its form; it follows the action quite freely, and only Leporello's leap of a seventh serves as a kind of connecting link by its frequent return in one guise or another. The harmony, too, follows the same fundamental principle: the bright lustre of E, B and F sharp major is dimmed fleetingly only at moments of emotional climax which foreshadow the final conflict.

Donna Anna's next scene (No. 25) is dramatically one of the weaknesses of the opera. It was probably included to allow more time for the setting of the final scene, which requires the whole depth of the stage. Mozart made a virtue of necessity by using the stop-gap to give a final touch to the development of Donna Anna's character immediately before Don Giovanni's downfall, and at the same time to achieve an extremely effective contrast with both the preceding and following scenes. Ottavio, it is true, remains as problematic as ever; his first words suggest that he has actually appealed to the law, but his essential feelings and thoughts are, as before, all centred on his love for Donna Anna.[1]

Before the aria there is a recitativo accompagnato which, like its Italian models,[2] anticipates the main themes in the first part of the aria. In form and general treatment, particularly the almost soloistic writing for the woodwind and the ample use of coloratura, it is nearer to the conventional Italian type than any other aria in the opera, yet at the same time the musical characterization is preserved.[3] Ottavio's renewed pleading awakens Donna Anna's tenderness, which helps her to accomplish to perfection what is,

---

[1] At one time his presence used to be replaced by a letter he had written to Donna Anna, which only made the situation more obscure without being of any help to him (hence the title: '(letter aria'). Kalbeck made him report that he had challenged Don Giovanni to a duel, which provided a better motive for Donna Anna's refusal to marry him at once.

[2] Jomelli's *Fetonte* includes an early example.

[3] It is entitled 'Rondo' in the same sense as many earlier concert arias.

after all, a very difficult task: to assure him of her love and yet refuse him his ultimate desire. She is still conscious of her duty to her murdered father, but as already shown, it has gradually turned into melancholy resignation, without losing any of its inner conviction. Here it accords with her affection for Ottavio and produces a secret conflict in her soul. A character such as hers cannot contemplate a division of loyalties: she cannot give herself to her bridegroom so long as her father is not avenged. This she announces to Don Ottavio with a wonderful delicacy that is truly Mozartian and allows both her affection and her secret anguish to shine through. The main theme, with the leading note descending to the fifth and the movement in octaves in the violins and violas, proclaims a touching sincerity of feeling, without any trace of sentimentality; the concluding section which introduces quite new material is also typical of Mozart. Here, as she openly expresses her love to Don Ottavio, the sound becomes perceptibly more eloquent, in the urgent Paisiello-like orchestral theme[1] and the way in which the woodwind take over her coloratura. The tender subsidiary theme in the clarinets also introduces her plea to Ottavio, in which her inner distress breaks through in quite modern terms:

Se— di— duol— non vuoi ch'io mo - ra, non vuoi ch'io mo - ra

The recapitulation leaves out this subsidiary theme completely and also considerably shortens the second section of the main group, which greatly enhances the effect of its modulations.

Then follows the Allegretto moderato, which must on no account be taken too fast. For Anna's first sentiment — hope that Heaven will sympathize with her in her need — we have been well prepared by what has gone before. At first she reveals her feelings quietly and discreetly; the continuation of the string theme by the wind is very expressive. Then the voice has a florid passage which was probably written for the benefit of the singer but should not be condemned because of the present hostile attitude towards coloratura in general. For without doubt it serves to express hope, rising radiantly and gradually sinking back again; the constantly fluctuating harmony with its interrupted cadences and six-five

---

[1] The beginning on the fifth instead of the third is, however, Mozartian.

chords somehow suspends it in the air, until finally the six-four chord of F major is reached and savoured to the full. Everything depends on *how* the passage is sung!

Immediately afterwards, incidentally, Donna Anna's old energy shows itself again in the syncopated passage with which she ends, after a short moment of melancholy reflection. This aria has often been misunderstood, but it is an essential part of the portrayal of Anna's character.

The construction of the second Finale (No. 26)[1] shows considerable dramatic and poetic skill. Once again we see Don Giovanni and his shadow Leporello, surrounded by material pleasures.[2] From the very beginning a glittering D major envelopes us in the festive atmosphere of a grand banquet of the time. Then the resident orchestra strikes up, as on all such occasions in Vienna; in this case it is a wind band, the sound of whose instruments is in

---

[1] This scene is much more diffuse in Gazzaniga's opera. It begins first of all with a secco recitative, while the first piece of music is the 'Concertino' of the *Tafelmusik*. Its beginning:

is in the style of the Viennese serenade; the middle section has oboe solo passages in the French style with the violins on the bass line. Then follows a recitativo accompagnato, and only at Don Giovanni's words 'Far devi un brindisi alla città' does the actual finale begin (Allegro non tanto 3/4, C major). Pasquariello's toast to the city of Venice and its beautiful ladies follows (Andante sotto voce 4/4, C major, with a solemn flourish in the horns). Then the knocking of the stone guest is heard, and Lanterna announces him, shaking with fear (Andante 4/4, D major then Allegro 4/4, A major). A recitative accompagnato (Largo, D minor, as with Mozart) precedes the entry of the ghost who begins his speech in a sombre E flat major. Here the contrast with Mozart is especially marked. True, the tempo is quicker, but the ghost's speech has not the same forceful impact; it proceeds in short accompagnati the effect of which is far less striking. Don Giovanni's downfall ensues in an E flat major movement entitled 'Furia', after which the complete ensemble finishes the opera in a cheerful Allegro (4/4, G major) as mentioned earlier (p. 37).

[2] Mozart, in his fragment of translation, mentions beautiful girls to dance to the *Tafelmusik*. There is nothing about them either in the score or in the libretto. In any case they would not be allowed to take part in the meal itself, being there merely for decoration. Don Giovanni does not say a word about them, which is in itself remarkable, and it seems justifiable to have left them out in more recent times.

itself humorous in colour. Here again we have a 'musical joke' but of a far more subtle kind, and it seems quite plausible that the idea of the *Tafelmusik* occurred to Mozart only during the rehearsals. The first two pieces that are played are pretty monotonous trifles from the operas mentioned, which for that very reason had become great popular favourites – Mozart knew his public well. More witty, though, is the frivolous reinterpretation of the texts in terms of the present, down to earth situation; when the voices occasionally move in unison with the tune it sounds as if they were ridiculing the old parodies that Mozart knew, after all, from the manuscript books of his youth. But then the musicians oblige with a theme from *Figaro*. Here again, the portrait of Cherubino, the young aristocrat, is transferred in a delightful manner to the greedily munching Leporello and so to the chef in praise of his excellent cuisine.

Thus the intervention of the supernatural is preceded by a mundane picture of a thoroughly ordinary day in the life of a nobleman. Don Giovanni and his servant are so engrossed in their eating, drinking and music that they have long forgotten the statue. But when Elvira appears the mood suddenly changes. The 'last token of her love' that she wants to give Don Giovanni, whose frivolous behaviour makes it even more difficult for her, is to warn him of the consequences of his deeds – consequences she clearly foresees since her nature is so close to his.[1] The conception is the same as Molière's: in her anxiety for her lover's life, her affection is such that she only wishes to save him from annihilation. The idea is as simple as it is beautiful, and one should guard against labelling her as another Gretchen, which would be completely alien to Mozart's way of thinking. With true psychological insight he has not reduced Elvira's passionate nature to a lofy resignation, but, on the contrary, extended it to an undreamt-of intensity – what a contrast to Donna Anna's development! In breathless haste, mostly in disjointed phrases which often sound more like cries, the melodic line sweeps along, urged on by Don Giovanni's resistance to ever new displays of passion. Nowhere else in the opera does her closeness to his elemental nature emerge

---

[1] That she wants to 'see him die as a penitent' (Schurig) is simply not supported by the text.

so clearly; it is as if a part of his own being had risen up against him.

Don Giovanni summons up all his strength to fight this un-expected opposition. His superiority expresses itself in icy scorn, and only his equally disconnected fragments of melody betray the fact that he, too, is in a state of great agitation. His derision is all the more frightening because he never descends so far as to be offensive; even here, he remains the perfect aristocrat. His mockery reaches a climax in a theme, several times repeated, which stands out against the otherwise rich orchestral sound with its own two-part writing:

This amounts almost to a popular ditty.[1] It is also noteworthy that Don Giovanni never refers to Elvira's words. First he invites her to dine with him, then he drinks the health of all women — that is all that remains of the traditional toast.

Musically the piece is a brilliant example of Mozart's free hand-ling of form, one of these movements which grow directly out of the dramatic situation and yet never violate the laws of musical architecture. He achieves this by the free repetition of each of the principal themes which he constantly spins out in new ways. The orchestra also contributes to the musical unity with a rhythmic motif: ♪ ♫♫♪ | ♩ that appears in a variety of melodic forms. This is complementary to the powerful basic rhythm of the voice parts, which move mostly in even crotchets. The declama-tion all through is syllabic, except for two florid passages on 'pie-tade' and 'cangi' in which Elvira seems to concentrate all her emotion on to one focal point, and the gloomy murmuring of Leporello ('Se non si muore' etc), who feels real pity for Elvira.

---

[1] In fact Mozart falls back, consciously or otherwise, on folklore. Dreysser's *Dantzbüchlein* of 1720 contains the following dance:

There is a still older melodic turn popular in 16th century songs, for example in Schein:

Finally the harmonic structure too is homogeneous, never venturing beyond the dominant; the harmonic foundation begins to shake only at Elvira's final scream. All the more powerful is the effect, within these narrow confines, of features such as the upward surge in the basses at the very beginning, with the subsequent pedal note and the decisive turn to the dominant on Elvira's coloratura. Psychologically her first, breathless words could not have been presented with greater subtlety and urgency. After the preceding episode for wind band the entry of the full orchestra (though without the festive trumpets and drums of the opening of the Finale) is in itself a dramatic event.

The dynamics are also remarkable: the whole piece is rich in sudden changes from forte to piano, in sforzato effects and short crescendos leading to piano; this is real Mozart, speaking in the strong, passionate language that he built up from its Mannheim foundations. Only once is there a crescendo of greater intensity: in the frightening passage when, for eleven bars, Elvira rends the air with her accusations against Don Giovanni on top F, at first together with its lower octave, while he boisterously repeats his praise of women. Here the conflict works up to a terrible climax; the whole orchestra is also in a state of wild excitement, so that the effect of Don Giovanni's cynicism is all the more cutting. By now his master's attitude is too much even for Leporello. His sympathy for Elvira draws him closer to her, and his quaver passage after the return of the opening clearly shows the impression her tremendous fate has made on him.

As Elvira screams the picture changes. In an agitated chromatic ascent the orchestra storms on to a diminished chord on B which, both in itself and through the syncopation associated with it, points forward to the ghostly music that is to follow. The whole episode is repeated and is leading up to the fatal key of D minor. But it is not yet time for this: between the two crucial movements Mozart once again interposes his comic character.[1] This F major episode, with its hammering pedal note, the quivering of the violins and the chromatic accompaniment in sixths in the wind, while leading away from the excitement of what has gone before, increases it even more effectively because

---

[1] Leporello also introduced the death scene of the Commendatore at the beginning of the first act.

124

tragedy is presented here in comic form. The way Leporello now expresses his fear is very different from his behaviour in, for example, the Sextet. Terror has completely paralysed his usually voluble tongue, and Don Giovanni's violent interjections stand out all the more sternly against his stammering. As the stone guest knocks at the door he can only shiver at each blow, and Don Giovanni has to seize the initiative in a sombre passage which seems at last to remind him of his invitation, while Leporello, with the same melody, crawls under the table.

After this masterly preparation, which carries the listener from the bustle of everyday life across the heights and depths of human passion to the very gates of eternity, the stone guest now enters with a shattering sound.[1] The power that he symbolizes is far removed from Don Giovanni's sphere in every respect. It knows no earthly emotions, neither anger, pity nor love. The instinctive drive that has so far led Don Giovanni to victory everywhere, is powerless against this opponent, and so the outcome of the battle between daemon and deamon is a foregone conclusion. Despite this, Don Giovanni rises to real tragic greatness in the energy with which he ventures his whole being, going to the uttermost limits of his strength. Even in his downfall he has more than human dimensions, and we are shaken by the massive power and frightfulness of the event itself, without having to look beyond it for a hint of divine justice.

---

[1] The entry of the trombones poses a problem which to this day has not really been solved. They do not appear in the autograph. However, that is no proof of their unauthenticity, for in numerous old scores the brass parts are written on separate sheets. In this case no such sheets are extant, either for the trombones or for the trumpets or timpani, but Rietz reports that in 1834 and 1836 he saw one in Mozart's handwriting in André's possession and had often held it in his hand; in 1865, at Mme Viardot's, he was deploring the loss of it. The Prague copy from Bassi's estate includes trombones. Gugler tried to prove that they were added later for Vienna, not by Mozart but by Süssmayer, whose handwriting is known to have been very like Mozart's. It is hardly thinkable that the supposed addition by Süssmayer would subsequently have been inserted into the original score. Among more recent scholars, Merian agrees with Gugler without furnishing new proof, and Jahn considers the trombones authentic, while Schurig evades the question, as does Komorzynski (*Mozart's Art of Instrumentation*), simply accepting the trombones as authentic.

We have already spoken of the general character of the Commendatore's music when discussing the overture. The massive pathos of its rigid rhythms and its melody, now resting on a single note, now moving in large, powerful intervals, is reminiscent of Gluck, whose style Mozart had already approached in *King Thamos*. The melody is constantly supported by the weighty rhythm ♩ ♪♩. ♪♩. sometimes in the whole orchestra, sometimes in the bass alone, although the full orchestra is always involved when the Commendatore is singing. It pauses only for short periods, and then in order to re-enter with redoubled force, as at the passage 'non si pasce di cibo mortale' with its strangely austere unison effect, and again at the words 'dammi la mano in pegno', where the mysterious G minor chord suddenly flares up in a wild fortissimo. At the same time the orchestral writing is full of colourful nuances. The rising and falling scale passages, for instance, already familiar from the overture, only now reveal their full expressive power at the words 'altre cure più grave' and, supported by unusually urgent harmonies, create an awe-inspring presentiment of the eternal.

The part played by Don Giovanni is in the sharpest contrast. His consternation at the arrival of his sinister guest, whom he had previously taken for an illusion and quite forgotten, is clearly mirrored in the syncopation and the murmuring figure in the second violins, transmitting itself also to the quaking Leporello. But as soon as he speaks for the second time, their paths diverge: while Don Giovanni, admittedly making an effort, enquires after the ghost's wishes, Leporello's teeth are already chattering in a triplet passage. Altogether the part he plays in this life and death struggle is perhaps the highest achievement of Mozart's skill in combining tragic and comic elements, and a profound, though gruesome, way of presenting tragedy in a comic form. For Leporello prattles away, not only between the words of his master but also between those of the ghost.

The Commendatore presses his point more and more strongly. In the massive chromatic ascent through the boldest of harmonic sequences his figure seems to grow to gigantic proportions, and once more Don Giovanni shivers.[1] But soon afterwards he, too,

---

[1] In da Ponte's text we find at this point a relic of older versions of the

rises to his full stature. While the ghost, leaping frightful intervals, sings his 'risolvi! verrai?' and Leporello again adds his indescribable:

Di - te di nò, di - te di nò!

Don Giovanni announces his final decision over that strangely harsh orchestral passage in dotted rhythms. Here in his full fury is the Don Giovanni behind the seducer who is apt to be forgotten; the champion of unbounded sensual urges, who prefers his own destruction to the surrender of even the smallest part of his power.

After this decision begins the Più stretto, for which Mozart has kept his strongest trumps in reserve. The atmosphere changes perceptibly here, if only because speech and counter-speech follow each other in short phrases, and in the end become only exclamations. The dotted rhythm appears only in the part of the Commendatore and of Don Giovanni who, after suppressing another fit of trembling, summons up every ounce of strength, and approaches the same plane of expression as his super-human adversary. Thus the contest of the two forces assumes proportions beyond anything known on earth. What is being enacted here is far more than punishment for a crime; it is a primaeval destiny that overwhelms us with the fury of a thunderstorm. All this is accompanied by dreadful onslaughts in the woodwind and brass over timpani rolls and tremolo strings. Below in the basses, on the other hand, mighty scales surge incessantly upwards. They may indeed bring to mind the analogous passage in the first act duel,[1] but they differ from it quite markedly, for not only do they not appear in imitation, but there is also the following characteristic leap of a seventh:

f   p

so that one cannot really speak of an intentional allusion.

Again the dynamics are full of sharp contrasts, without any crescendos; it is only the change from 'f' to 'p' that becomes

---

legend, namely the stone guest's invitation to Don Giovanni, which brings about the latter's downfall. This is not consistent with da Ponte's continuation, in which Don Giovanni's end occurs in his own house immediately after the statue disappears.

---

[1] According to Bulthaupt.

more and more frequent. Leporello exclaims his 'si! si!' only once more in this section, just before the moment of decision. Immediately afterwards come the two mighty blows of Don Giovanni's ultimate 'No!', followed by the sinister pp unison passage of the statue before it disappears.

This is the point at which the conflict comes to a head. The Allegro represents the voice of the Inferno, with a male unison chorus in the style of Gluck. In the bass line the dotted rhythm of the statue still booms on, but then the orchestra devotes itself entirely to the description of the the upheaval that is taking place in nature, in fiery turns of phrase and wildly tugging syncopation. The fact that nature now raises its voice signifies far more than an external increase of intensity. It lends the Finale an almost mythical quality, and with a sense of trepidation we feel the oneness of fate, nature and man. After Don Giovanni's disappearance the storm subsides in a beautiful plagal cadence, its fury still vibrating softly in the chromatic lines of the inner parts. A mighty crescendo leads to the D major chord which produces an incomparable effect, not in the sense of a 'happy' resolution, but as an expression of cold pitiless majesty.[1]

To this day this part of the Finale is regarded as one of the highlights of musical drama, not to be surpassed. Jahn's comment is pertinent: 'The mood of the sublime and the supernatural to which we submit without reserve is so securely maintained all through a comparatively long scene that the listener is carried away in Mozart's grip, soaring clear-eyed above the abyss in breathless suspense.' One has to make sure, however, that the shattering impact of the music is not weakened by spectacular stage effects such as fireworks, devilish masks, conflagrations, the collapse of the palace etc. In Prague the technical equipment of the theatre precluded anything of the kind, but theatrical directors soon seized upon this 'grateful' scene and loaded it with various crude effects borrowed from popular plays;[2] later on, the engineering skills of romantic opera were brought into play, Don Giovanni's

---

[1] Rightly recognized by A. Heuss. This impression is created by the almost exclusive use of minor keys beforehand.

[2] At a performance in Berne in 1810, panic broke out when the six devils engaged for the occasion were joined by a self-appointed seventh; two of them came to grief.

house was made to fall in, the churchyard with the equestrian statue reappeared, and so on.

All this is partly bound up with the question of what attitude one should adopt towards the movements of the Finale that are still to follow. It was soon recognized that after the ghost scene they present a difficult problem. The original score suggests cutting the Larghetto in so far as it deals only with the personal affairs of those concerned.[1] Mozart must therefore have toyed with the idea of at least shortening the scene, even in Prague. In Vienna he wanted to bring the pursuers on to the stage at the last moment, to utter a cry of horror on the D major chord; but he rejected this too, and we do not know whether the idea was ever carried out.[2] In any case, the opera finished on this occasion with the catastrophic end of Don Giovanni, as it generally did later on. An exception was the Dresden Opera, which until 1836 included the complete Finale.

In the romantic era there were, however, most unfortunate attempts to change the final scene altogether. At a performance in Paris, after Don Giovanni's fall, Donna Anna's coffin was surrounded by a group of mourners who sang the 'Dies Irae' from Mozart's *Requiem*.[3] Kugler suggested that the scene should be changed to the Commendatore's memorial chapel, and that for his funeral rites the chorus should sing again from the Requiem, 'Lux eterna luceat ei (not 'eis' since there was only one person), domine, cum sanctis tuis quia pius es'. Then the 'Osanna in excelsis' would make a 'suitable' ending. To crown everything, Schurig proposed that Don Giovanni and Leporello should rush to the churchyard after the ghost has vanished, to see whether the statue is still standing on its pedestal; they find that it is, illuminated in a fantastic manner. From the vaults pious chants are heard. Don Giovanni, racked by the fire within him, finally dies 'unrepenting' while Leporello 'kneels in prayer'; day breaks and the pious chants are heard again. One really cannot ask for more

---

[1] Gugler assumes that Süssmayer is the author of this cut.
[2] Rietz is of the opinion that the final ensemble must have been left out in Prague, since the Commendatore and Masetto were played by the same singer, and there would have been no time for him to change his costume.
[3] Viol is also in favour of this funeral scene, but with the music of Mozart's original ending (!!)

in the way of up-to-date 'atmosphere'. The only thing that remains completely obscure is what music Schurig had in mind.

Let this catalogue of sins committed against the end of the opera suffice to show that no modern school of thought has any reason to be proud of its sense of style. We have no right to distort Mozart's masterpiece by a stagey finish, either in the manner of Meyerbeer or in the most modern taste. Seriously speaking, there can be only two alternatives: the complete original Finale, or else ending with the descent to Hell. Dramatically nothing can be said against the second of these, for we are sufficiently informed about the fate of the other characters and the opera would finish with its greatest climax. Admittedly it means that the tragic aspect would have the last word. The most recent performers, however, in accordance with contemporary interest in historical and stylistic accuracy, have tended to return to the complete Finale, with a strong accent on opera buffa. This is prompted by the probably correct feeling, that after the gruesome nocturnal trio the opera needs a reassuring end. At the same time such an ending can only be justified if it leads the whole work to an organic conclusion. In this we can expect no help from so-called historical accuracy, which in this instance would turn the opera into something purely artistic; nor from the unadulterated buffo style, which would reduce Mozart's whole conception of the last scene to the manner of the Italians whom he had long surpassed. There is really no need for any extraneous reasons to vindicate this ending, if only one keeps Mozart's conception clearly in mind.

What does happen in these three movements? After the death of Don Giovanni all his victims come together, describe the impression it has made on them, and then draw practical conclusions for the future. The only feeling that remains with them is moral satisfaction that virtue has won the final victory. Da Ponte intended this scene, in which the everyday world sits in judgement over the extraordinary, to be taken quite seriously, as we saw.[1] If Mozart, after the nocturnal battle between the daemons, lets the bright, everyday sun shine again, he does so with the ironic humour characteristic of his whole dramatic technique. This is seen most clearly in the strongly contrasting figures of Leporello

---

[1] cf p. 41.

DON GIOVANNI

and Don Ottavio. Leporello, whom these momentous events have
passed by without taking the slightest notice of him, is to be the
one who reports on them, not without pride — he, the arch-
philistine, telling of his extraordinary master. But after this report
Ottavio pours out a new love song as if nothing had happened, and
has to be content with being put off by Donna Anna for yet
another year! It is not as if this final scene suddenly put them all
on the same level: on the contrary, as Donna Anna shows us, they
remain on different dramatic planes. But the basic feeling remains
the same with all of them, merely expressing itself in different
ways. At the end, the ecclesiastical nature of the Presto even
suggests something like a religious ceremony, in which hearts beat
faster at the thought of divine retribution. Thus Mozart smiles
down ironically once again on his own creations; he too feels their
perplexities, but presents them from a more exalted viewpoint.

Understood in this way, the three movements lose the character
of mere appendices stuck on at the end; they round off the opera
organically in a genuinely Mozartian way. Thus the reproach so
frequently heard that they 'fall off musically when compared with
what has gone before' is untenable. The sphere in which we now
find ourselves could never support such other-worldly flights of
the imagination as in the previous scene. Mozart has no intention
of weakening the effect of the ending, which grows in its own
distinctive way once again from the framework as a whole, quite
differently from the shallow closing scenes of the Italians.

Again, the three movements are clearly connected with one
another; the first and third are predominantly for the whole
ensemble, the second is for the individual soloists. This is basically
the principle of the French vaudeville, except that the three
sections are quite independent. The first, whose key of G major
is fore-shadowed in the preceding plagal cadence, is in a fresh
lively vein that leads after a somewhat conventional opening to
more and more individual treatment, beginning with Leporello's
narration. Here some echoes of the appalling catastrophe can still
be heard, particularly the impression it has made on the others; in
the last eleven bars they are clearly overcome by terror. The
Larghetto is a piece of enchanting beauty, which at first brings
Donna Anna and Ottavio to the fore. But the irony of Ottavio's

131

happiness being once more put off for a year is further reinforced by the fact that Elvira's words, immediately afterwards, introduce a buffo element which at 'resti dunque quel birbon con Proserpina e Pluton' even verges on parody. The way in which the three less distinguished characters finally turn to the easy-going folksong style of the 'antichissima canzon' is very attractive. But the two noble ladies take the words out of their mouths. The last thing Mozart wanted was to finish the opera in the buffo vein of his Italian predecessors, with the performers advancing to the footlights and taking off their masks with a smile. He also gives Don Giovanni's antagonists their dramatic due in a stirring individual section that grips the listener at once. As to the affinity with a more austere style of sacred music, it is carried only so far as is demanded by the fundamental design of the whole scene, already described.[1]

Of the numbers added later for the Vienna performance, Ottavio's aria (No. 11) is dramatically so weak as to be almost damaging.[2] It conflicts with the preceding recitative in which Ottavio talks of his duty to take vengeance, quite apart from the fact that it is out of place after the tragedy that has befallen Donna Anna. Certainly such an outpouring of affection is fundamentally in keeping with the character of the man, yet it is not at all like Mozart to insert an aria in this abrupt way, without regard to the dramatic situation. Obviously he was not free to do as he pleased in adapting the opera for Vienna. Whether he was considering the singers or the Viennese public's liking for languishing lovers, must remain a matter of opinion. Apart from that basic defect the aria is of course one of Mozart's most beautiful love songs, transfiguring the tender Italian type, without any false

---

[1] The final section of the Quartet in *Die Entführung* is constructed in a similar way, even to the accompanying figures and scale passages in the violins. The long sustained chord on the word 'morte' and the pedal note on 'sempre ugual' are also reminiscent of sacred music.

[2] Vincent's suggestion that it should go before the Quartet in the first act (omitting the recitative) has been accepted by Wolzogen, Gradaur and Kalbeck, without effecting much improvement. There is no alternative but to transfer the aria from the theatre to the concert platform. The Gesamtausgabe, incidentally, is inconsistent in putting it in the text, like Elvira's aria (No. 23), instead of relegating it, like the duet 'Per queste tue manine', to the appendix.

sentiment. Moreover, the binary form is shaped with character-istic freedom. The first part uses the whole text, while the very Italianate G minor episode with the 'sospiri' in the woodwind is treated as the second and more intense section, which then leads back to the beginning by means of a most ingenious modulation through B minor. The second part no longer refers to the 'sospiri', but develops only the main theme, extending it most poetically. The short coda, in which the voice momentarily doubles the bass line, is also beautifully effective.

The other alterations for Vienna — the addition of the duet between Leporello and Zerlina 'Per queste tue manine' and of Donna Elvira's well known aria (No. 23) are no better; Ottavio's aria (No. 22) was left out. The duet is not only dramatically out of place, but from the purely musical point of view quite insignifi-cant; there is not a single detail that would make one think of Mozart. Elvira's aria, on the other hand, dramatically only a stop-gap and in any case understandable in its context only as an insertion,[1] does at least make a musically attractive piece, even if it does not quite fit in with the picture of Elvira's character. Psychologically it can certainly be argued that her former passion-ate desire to win back her lover might turn to pity for the doomed man: but this attitude does not in any way fit Elvira's true nature. She would be much more likely to express her struggle with all its contradictions and to fight her way through with characteristic fire, than to content herself with this strangely meek acceptance of mental anguish.

Only the recitative alludes to her inner conflict, and certainly the gradual change the main motif undergoes from violent emotion to resigned grief[2] is a particularly beautiful example of Mozart's genius for accompagnato writing. The aria itself is a fully-fledged rondo, but the opportunities for contrast inherent in this form are

---

[1] Elvira has now heard about Don Giovanni's latest iniquity. But if this scene is omitted, as it should be, the aria is left in mid-air. It is not appro-priate as a reply to Ottavio's aria either, and Rochlitz's suggestion that it should be sung after Leporello's 'catalogue' aria is most unfortunate. It would also be unsuitable after the 'letter' aria, as Schurig proposed. So once more there is nothing left but to relegate it to the concert platform.

[2] This matches the recitative itself, with its heroic opening and strange, ques-tioning end.

not exploited at all. On the contrary, the piece is in one mood throughout, the main theme returning constantly. Its essential feature is a continuous quaver movement that creates agitation without purpose and without contrasts. The chief feature of all these insertions – their dependence on existing formulae – applies no less to this aria; the outline of the main theme itself would have been very familiar to Italian ears. On the other hand, the 'concertante' character of the accompaniment already foreshadows *Così fan tutte.*

The secco recitatives, like those in *Figaro*, belong throughout to the buffo style and have therefore the same principal features. But sometimes they are even more strikingly individual than in the earlier work – for instance, in expressing a question through the melody finishing on the third (the most obvious example), or by using the chord of the second, or by an interrupted cadence with a freely entering bass.[1] By contrast, the ending of some of the recitatives acquires added impact through the bass reaching the tonic not by the stereotyped interval of a fifth, but by step, from the supertonic. It is in this arresting way that Zerlina introduces her first aria and Elvira the Sextet.

In keeping with the nature of the drama, the harmonic structure of the secco recitatives is altogether more pertinent and more austere than in *Figaro*. The Gluckian style of declamation, such as the rising melodic sequences over a chromatically ascending bass in situations of mounting excitement, is far more frequent than in *Figaro*, even in an almost comic sense – for example, after the Sextet when the characters all converge one after another on the wretched Leporello. In such cases Mozart also had a liking for chords of the second with their resolution, often to the extent of writing several one after another. A typical example of his way of harmonizing secco recitatives in emotional passages is Elvira's impassioned speech after her first aria: 'Cosa puoi dire dopo azion si nera?' etc., up to the Phrygian close; so, in a different way, is the short recitative before Ottavio's interpolated aria, where the idea of the 'nero delitto' produces the otherwise very rare chord of

---

[1] The 'Phrygian question' occurs even in *Don Giovanni* only once, significantly in Elvira's part ('che t'amai cotanto'), and then not as a question but as a reproach.

134

the diminished seventh. His B flat major aria, too, is preceded by a recitative with highly evocative harmonies. Finally, before the Quartet (No. 9), when Don Giovanni has composed himself, he moves further and further into the flat keys till Elvira cuts him short emphatically. This very effective procedure is certainly intentional.

It frequently happens that the calm of the bass line is interrupted by lively little motifs, though not, as in *Figaro*, for long stretches. Some of them serve to underline the emotional atmosphere, but most illustrate a musical gesture or prepare a particular event.

All these examples show that, within the limits defined by the style of the 'secco', Mozart was striving once again to distinguish the individual characters one from another. The dialogue between master and servant in the cemetery is typical of this. It simply bubbles out (almost entirely in semiquavers!), as they throw remarks to one another, back and forth like tennis balls, calling for a lively use of gesture. Only occasionally is the feeling stronger, tinged with irony, as when Don Giovanni sings 'Leporello mio caro'. Don Giovanni has his own peculiar way of declaiming, which distinguishes him from the others even in the 'secco'. Here, too, he is always superior, whether expressing his domineering nature or his exuberant spirits. The idea in the 'secco' of setting the syntactically important words to the notes of the underlying chord is particularly marked in his case, as for example at the beginning of the cemetery scene mentioned above:

This simple, one might almost say fanfare-like, melody is characteristic of Don Giovanni. On one occasion it is even caricatured most delightfully by Leporello:

Rhythmically as well, Don Giovanni's speeches are always definite and forceful; for example, a particularly violent effect is produced when, as he is beating up Masetto, the passage:

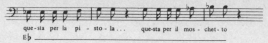

is immediately repeated a tone higher. By comparison, Leporello's melodic line is much less striking, unless he happens to feel in command of the situation and tries to imitate his master.[1] Rhythmically, his part has a restless and prattling quality, with a tendency to move in semiquavers. Only when he has to read the inscription does he rise to greater pathos.

Of the women, Elvira's characterization is the most acute in the 'secco'. The harmonic treatment corresponds to the melodic structure which, in sharp contrast to Don Giovanni's lapidary style, is much more complex and tortuous. Consider, for example, the passage immediately before the Quartet in the first act:

In the third 'secco' of the second act she even has, at the words 'mio tesoro!', a small, sighing suspension. Her emotional nature also shows itself again and again in enormously varied and excited rhythms. Donna Anna does not, on the whole, have a large share in the 'secco'; she expresses herself rather in the 'accompagnato' and in the arias and ensembles. On the other hand, Don Ottavio's tender nature comes through quite clearly in the 'secco', and Zerlina's naïveté also stands out against the style of Don Giovanni as well as that of Masetto.

These recitatives, therefore, also contribute to the cohesion of the whole. Of course it is essential, as always, that the performers should not only have assimilated their roles completely, but also be thoroughly versed in the 'action'. Obviously Italian secco recitative will never flourish quite as well when translated into any other language.[2] Nevertheless, with the right kind of schooling considerably more could be achieved than some theatres[3] in our

---

[1] This is very much the case when he addresses Elvira before his catalogue aria.

[2] Abert literally says, 'in the German language'. (P.G.)

[3] Literally 'some German theatres'. (P.G.)

own time have managed. The once popular substitution of spoken dialogue for the 'secco' only replaces one evil with another and in more recent times has quite rightly been almost universally abandoned.

That Mozart could, within a year, create two masterpieces such worlds apart in their aims and content as *Figaro* and *Don Giovanni,* is supreme proof of the universal nature of his genius. *Figaro* unfolds, despite all its fleeting shadows, as a fundamentally bright picture of a world that enjoys its existence, and is, moreover, illuminated by the shimmering sunset of an aristocratic culture; at the same time it closes a quite distinct phase in Mozart's development, which had found its purest expression in the piano concertos. *Don Giovanni,* on the other hand, was preceded by works like the first two string quintets, in which Mozart writes far less for the sake of his public than in order to satisfy his own compulsion to create; his artistic bond with the outside world is loosened, and even though he continues working to order, he follows his own inner voice more and more. With his health already beginning to decline, he now retires into himself and reflects on all kinds of problems. His last letter to his father, in which he meditates on death, has recently been related to the contemporaneous composition of *Don Giovanni*; rightly so, though in this context the opera must be regarded as a complement to the letter. For to his father Mozart presents death as a benevolent friend, while the music of *Don Giovanni* reveals all its terrors. Clearly at this time he must have lived through hours when, despite all the teachings of Freemasonry, the sensual side of his nature, the side akin to Goethe, was stirring within him.

This change of attitude explains why he no longer concentrates his main effort, as in *Figaro*, on presenting with an ironic smile the interplay of spiritual forces in the human tragi-comedy. What fascinates him now is its fatal aspect. So he succeeds in raising everything to an extraordinary level, intensifying every passion to breaking point, even summoning transcendental powers with whom he may well have communicated at this time in many a quiet hour. While in the music of *Figaro* we sense the heart-warming joy of its creator, that of *Don Giovanni* springs from a tremendous energy that has only one aim, to exhaust the potential of its material completely. It is quite understandable that at the time it seemed odd, even repulsive. This opera was no longer an 'amusement', even in the best sense, but held the listener in a continuous state of tension with its calculated, heartrending contrasts. There is a terrifying clarity of expression in the orchestration, which differs enormously from that of *Figaro*, especially in the dynamics, which here as in no other Mozart opera move between the most extreme limits and with scarcely any transitions. With terrible force this music storms across the heights and depths of human fortune; it leads us into a world so sublime that the heart stands still, and then plunges into the gloomy, fenced-in, workaday world, so as to force a smile from the public at the truthfulness of its portrayal. Mozart's skill in relating his characters to one another and in measuring against each other the worlds they represent, here achieves it greatest triumph; it is revealed as the main source of his inspired fusion of tragic and comic elements.

But with all this striving for realism there is never any violation or cheapening of the musical expression. The listener of the time was asked to accept a great deal, but nothing anti-musical. Though the form may often be handled with a freedom that gave conservative minds of the period some troubled moments, there is never any question of shapelessness, with Mozart of all composers! He only claimed the natural right of genius to find new forms for the new content of his experience. That he was perfectly conscious of what was necessary and appropriate in his art is self-evident. Even the fiercest outbursts of passion submit to his firm will to create and to shape, and to transform nature into supreme art.

Thus he produced a work that bears the same relation to its predecessors as Goethe's *Faust* to earlier adaptations of the Faust legend. The question as to whether it belongs to the field of tragic or comic opera never occurred to him, though it caused later commentators so much concern. For however many connexions *Don Giovanni* may have with opera buffa, it has become something of much greater significance. The materials may be the same, but the building that Mozart created with them is his own work, and a work of genius. It is useless to try and force it into a conventional mould; it is unique.